# IS PINE HOLLOW STABLES HAUNTED?

"That's not the first weird thing that's happened around here lately," Mrs. Reg said, shaking her head slowly. She sat down on the edge of a trunk, looking thoughtful. "Have you girls ever heard of poltergeists?"

"Sure," Lisa said promptly. "They're a sort of mischievous, playful ghost."

"Not always so playful," Mrs. Reg corrected. "They can be very destructive, if you believe the people who say they've been haunted by them. Like the people at Nevermore Stables. After almost a year of mysterious, annoying, sometimes dangerous mishaps—misplaced tack, unlatched gates, odd tapping and banging noises, things like that—they had no choice but to close down. The students were convinced it was a poltergeist at work, and they quit in droves."

"But that's ridiculous," Carole said. "Even the best-run stable has an occasional accident."

The worried crease in Mrs. Reg's forehead deepened. "Occasional, yes," she said softly. "But when the occasional becomes the everyday, well . . ."

# THE SADDLE CLUB

# HORSE MAGIC

## BONNIE BRYANT

A BANTAM SKYLARK BOOK
NEW YORK • TORONTO • LONDON • SYDNEY • AUCKLAND

RL 5, 009–012

HORSE MAGIC

A Bantam Skylark Book / September 1995

ISBN 0-553-48265-3

Published simultaneously in the United States and Canada

Bantam Books are published by Bantam Books, a division of Bantam Double-
day Dell Publishing Group, Inc. Its trademark, consisting of the words "Bantam Books" and the portrayal of a rooster, is Registered in U.S. Patent and
Trademark Office and in other countries. Marca Registrada. Bantam Books,
1540 Broadway, New York, New York 10036.

PRINTED IN THE UNITED STATES OF AMERICA

OPM    9  8  7  6  5

*I would like to express my special thanks
to Catherine Hapka
for her help in the writing of this book.*

"I'M GLAD YOU could come today, Phil," Carole Hanson said, leaning back against the wall of Pine Hollow Stables' indoor ring. "Mr. Toll's talk should be really interesting."

"I'm glad, too," Phil Marsten agreed. "Once in a while Stevie actually manages to come up with a good idea." He turned to grin at Stevie Lake, his girlfriend and one of Carole's two best friends.

Stevie replied by sticking out her tongue at him, and Carole laughed. It was a rainy Saturday morning in October, and in a few minutes it would be time for the weekly meeting of Pine Hollow's Pony Club, Horse Wise. This week's meeting was unmounted. When they were having a discussion instead of riding, Max allowed them to invite guests. Stevie had invited Phil, who rode at a stable in a neighboring town and belonged to a different Pony Club chapter there. The scheduled speaker was a local farmer named Mr. Toll who owned Clydesdales and other work-horses. These giant, hardworking beasts didn't have a whole lot in common with the riding horses at Pine Hollow, but they were still horses, and that was the most important thing of all, in Carole's opinion. She loved all horses. In fact, she and Stevie and their other best friend, Lisa Atwood, loved horses and riding so much that they had formed The Saddle Club. The group had only two rules: Members had to be horse-crazy, and they had to be willing to help each other out in any way necessary.

Carole could hardly wait to hear Mr. Toll speak. She had first met him when her father had hired the old farmer to take Carole and her friends on a hayride for her birthday. She knew that he was an expert on old-fashioned farming methods as well as on breeding and training workhorses. Carole was glad that Max Regnery, the owner of Pine Hollow and the girls' riding instructor, liked his students to be well rounded and learn everything they could about everything having to do with horses—from fox hunting to horse racing and from show grooming to basic veterinary care. It made their favorite subject even more interesting.

"I wonder where Lisa is?" Stevie said, interrupting Carole's thoughts. "It's not like her to be late."

As if on cue, Lisa hurried into the ring. She looked around until she spotted her friends, then hurried over and plopped down next to them. "Whew!" she exclaimed, red-faced and out of breath. "I thought I'd never get here."

"We thought so, too," Stevie replied. "What happened?"

"It was my mother's fault," Lisa began. That was no surprise to the others. Mrs. Atwood was the one who had first insisted that Lisa learn to ride. She thought it was one of the things every proper young lady should be able to do, along with needlepoint, ballet, piano, and about a dozen other boring things. It was definitely not part of Mrs. Atwood's plan for her daughter to become horse-crazy, but that was exactly what had happened. Since Lisa was a straight-A student who excelled at just about everything she did, she was already a very good rider, even though she hadn't been riding as long as Carole and Stevie had. Mrs. Atwood didn't exactly disapprove of her daughter's favorite hobby, but she didn't always understand why it was so important for Lisa to be on time for things like Horse Wise meetings.

"What did she do, stop along the way to sign you up for mambo lessons?" Stevie teased.

"Not exactly," Lisa said with a grin. "But I'm sure she would have if she'd thought of it. Actually, she had to stop at the dry cleaner's to pick up her Halloween costume. She and my dad are going to a party next weekend."

"What's the costume?" Carole asked, feeling a twinge of sadness. The three girls had decided the previous year that they were getting too old for trick-or-treating and wouldn't be dressing up anymore. Carole had agreed with the decision at the time, but now that the holiday was rolling around again she was starting to regret it. Dressing up for Halloween was an awful lot of fun. Carole had even come up with an idea for a costume before she remembered she wouldn't need it. It was too bad—she was sure her friends would have loved it.

Lisa rolled her eyes. "My mom wears the same costume every year—Cinderella."

The others laughed. That sounded like just the kind of costume Mrs. Atwood would like.

"Horse Wise, come to order!" With those words, Max strode into the ring, followed by two other adults. One of them was Mr. Toll. The other was a slim, pretty young woman wearing jeans and a patterned blouse.

"I wonder who that is," Stevie whispered to Phil. "She doesn't exactly look like a farmer's assistant."

"I know you're all looking forward to hearing Mr. Toll speak today," Max began. "But first I'd like to introduce you to a surprise guest who's going to take a few minutes to talk to you before Mr. Toll gets started. This is Susan Connors. She works with Deborah at the paper." Deborah Hale, Max's wife, was a reporter for a newspaper in nearby Washington, D.C.

"Hello, everyone," Susan Connors said when Max was finished. "Thanks for letting me speak to you today. I know you're all eager to get on with your meeting, so I'll be brief. I'm a volunteer for a nonprofit organization called City Kids/Country Kids."

"I've heard of that," Lisa whispered to her friends. "My parents have donated money to them."

"What we do," Susan continued, "is try to help disadvantaged kids in Washington, D.C. For one thing, we work with several other charity groups to distribute food, clothing, and other necessities. But in addition to taking care of their needs, we try to find ways for them to have fun. Because the neighborhoods where most of them live aren't always safe places to play, we sponsor trips to places that are. In the summer, for instance, we run a camp in the Blue Ridge Mountains. We also run several team sports leagues that play on the Mall in D.C. But besides those regular programs we're always looking for other places to take groups of kids—farms, national parks, anyplace we think will be fun for them."

Carole immediately raised her hand. "Maybe some of the kids could come here to Pine Hollow," she suggested eagerly. "I'm sure they'd love to see all the beautiful horses here, maybe even learn to ride . . ." Her voice trailed off when she glanced at Max, who looked annoyed. Biting her lip, she realized that he was probably mad at her for volunteering his stable without permission. Carole knew that her offer had been impetuous, but whenever there was a problem, she couldn't help trying to come up with a solution involving horses. The idea of bringing city kids to Pine Hollow for a day of fresh air and horses made perfect sense to her. Still, Max ran a pretty tight ship, and he might not like the idea of a bunch of strangers running around interrupting the routine.

But her fears were put to rest a second later when Max's expression changed into a rueful smile. "I should have known you'd jump the gun on my great idea, Carole," he said. "As a matter of fact, I've already volunteered Pine Hollow to Susan as the site for the group's Halloween party next Saturday."

"That's right," Susan said over the surprised gasps that greeted the announcement. "We had another site lined up, but it fell through. It's really great of Max to agree to this at the last minute." She smiled at Carole. "And it's nice to see that his riders are just as good-hearted as he is."

"They'd better be," Max said warningly, glancing at the young riders. "This event is going to take a lot of work to pull off. I'll need lots of help planning and running it, especially since I didn't realize when I volunteered that most of the younger riders here are going to be at their school party at the public elementary school. So you older kids are really going to have to pitch in and help."

The Saddle Club exchanged glances. Each of them knew exactly what the others were thinking. Without a word, they all raised their hands.

"We'd be happy to help out, Max," Stevie called. "We have some experience in this sort of thing, you know." The year before, the three girls had spent Halloween with their friend Kate Devine at her family's dude ranch out West. Mrs. Devine had asked them to come to help her plan a

Halloween fair benefiting the local school's American Indian program. The fair had been a huge success. The Saddle Club was sure they could do the same for this Halloween event.

"It's settled, then," Max said, nodding to The Saddle Club and the other Pony Clubbers who had raised their hands to volunteer. "Susan, you don't have to worry about a thing. With this group in control, those kids will have more fun than they can handle!"

"Great," Susan said with a smile. "That's exactly what we're trying to give them. Thanks a lot, everyone, and I'll see you next weekend!" With a cheerful wave, she headed out of the ring.

After she had gone, Phil raised his hand. "Max, I know I'm not a member of Horse Wise, but I'd love to help out next weekend," he said. "I even have an idea for something special I could do for the kids."

Max looked surprised, but he shrugged agreeably. "The more the merrier," he said. "What did you have in mind?"

"A Halloween magic show," Phil replied. "I'm a pretty good amateur magician, if I do say so myself, and it would be nice to perform for someone other than my sisters."

Stevie stared at him. She'd had no idea Phil could do magic tricks.

But Max looked pleased. "That's a terrific idea," he said. "We're going to have to come up with enough activities to keep a dozen or so kids occupied all day, and that could be a

7

challenge. A magic show should be a lot of fun. You're hired, Phil."

Suddenly a gruff voice spoke up. "Well now, if this is turning into some kind of community event, I think I'd better volunteer, too," said Mr. Toll.

Everyone turned to look at him in surprise. With all the excitement over Susan's visit, they had almost forgotten the old farmer was in the room.

"If these youngsters are going to have a real country Halloween, they're going to have to go trick-or-treating," Mr. Toll continued. "Might be fun for them to do it in a hay wagon—not so tiring that way."

"What a great idea!" Stevie exclaimed. "The hayride you gave us on Carole's birthday was so much fun—those city kids will love it!"

Mr. Toll just nodded, but the girls thought they could detect a twinkle of pleasure in his blue eyes. "It's settled, then," the farmer said gruffly. "Providin' this blasted rain stops by then, that is."

"Oh, it will," Stevie predicted confidently. "It wouldn't dare rain when we've got something so important to do." She looked a little surprised when everyone burst into laughter. It was typical of Stevie to assume that even the weather would automatically go along with her plans.

"Okay, everyone, settle down," Max said. "Let's have a quick planning meeting for the event after Mr. Toll's talk. Anyone who would like to volunteer to help next Saturday should stay."

Mr. Toll took over and began telling the students about his experiences farming the same land for more than sixty years. Despite her interest in the topic, Carole found her mind wandering back to the Halloween event. She knew that with The Saddle Club on the case it was certain to be a fun day for the city kids. Carole was glad to be able to help with such a worthy cause. Although she had lived on or near military bases all over the country because of her father's career in the Marine Corps, Carole had never lived in a big city. It was hard for her to imagine being somewhere where she wouldn't be able to ride and be around horses. She knew that the children Susan's group tried to help had a lot of very serious problems, and that not being able to ride was the least of them. Still, Carole was glad to think that horses might play a part in making the kids' lives a little more fun. One of the best things about horses, in Carole's opinion, was the way that just being around them seemed to help people in lots of different ways. Her mother had died when Carole was eleven years old, and riding was one of the things she could always count on to make her feel better. Horses and riding had also helped Carole and her friends many other times in many other ways.

Carole was brought back to reality by Lisa's asking a question. "Mr. Toll, how many workhorses do you have now?"

The farmer scratched his head, thinking. "Let's see, now," he drawled. "There's Dapper and Dan, my team of matched bay Clydesdales. Then I have another matched pair—no special breeding on them, just regular horses, but good, solid workers. They're twin brother and sister, both blacks, named Superstition and Black Magic."

"What a great idea!" Carole cried out. She blushed a little when everyone turned to look at her, but then she explained. "Sorry to interrupt, Mr. Toll. I was just thinking that a pair of black horses would be perfect for the Halloween event. Maybe they could pull the hay wagon."

Mr. Toll scratched his head again. "I sure don't see why not," he said. "They ain't as good-looking as the Clydesdales, but they're just as strong."

"It's perfect, Carole," Stevie agreed enthusiastically. "They've even got the perfect names for Halloween—Black Magic and Superstition."

"Funny you should mention that," Mr. Toll said. "Fact is, the names are a little bit of a joke. Back when that pair was born, there were some among the old country folk who thought I shouldn't even keep 'em."

Stevie and Lisa exchanged amused glances. In their opinion, Mr. Toll himself definitely qualified as one of the "old country folk."

"Why's that, Mr. Toll?" Carole asked.

"Because the both of them were born with four white feet," Mr. Toll replied. Seeing the mystified looks on most of the students' faces, he recited, " 'One white foot, buy him; two white feet, try him; three white feet, doubt him; four white feet—do without him!' It's an old superstition from the days when some folks still believed in black magic.

That's how I got the names—Superstition for the colt, Black Magic for the filly. 'Course they're not colt and filly anymore—they're going on twenty. But I still get a chuckle out of those names."

The Saddle Club had a hard time imagining solid, serious Mr. Toll chuckling at anything. But they loved his story nonetheless, and they were sure the city kids would love it, too. They made him promise to tell it to them on Halloween.

". . . AND I STILL can't believe you never mentioned you could do magic," Stevie exclaimed for the fifth time. She, Carole, and Lisa were keeping Phil company while he waited for his father to pick him up. All four of them were perched on the fence beside the driveway, discussing the Horse Wise meeting. The rain had finally stopped, and the girls had a few minutes before they had to get ready for their riding lesson.

"Forget it, Stevie," Carole advised her friend. "We've got more important things to think about—like how we're going to come up with enough costumes for twelve kids."

Lisa shook her head. "It's still kind of hard to believe these kids are so poor they can't even afford Halloween costumes," she said.

"I know," Carole agreed. "That's why it's so important that they all have a wonderful time on Saturday."

"Well, like Max said, they're sure to have more fun than they can handle with The Saddle Club helping plan things," Stevie said confidently. "Remember how great the Halloween fair was last year? We could do some of the same stuff again here. You know, like the costume contest, the candy corn contest—"

"Hold on a minute, Stevie," Lisa interrupted. "Even though all those things were fun, some of them were really mostly to raise money for the cause. This time we're not trying to raise money at all, just show a good time to a group of city kids."

"Hmm. I guess you're right," Stevie said. "But Max obviously thinks we can do it. That's why he put us in charge of the entertainment. We should be able to come up with plenty to do—you can hardly help having fun on Halloween."

"True," Carole said, remembering her earlier thoughts. She smiled. Now she'd get a chance to wear her costume after all!

"Besides," Stevie continued, "if anyone can show those kids a good time on Halloween, it's me. After all, I am the undisputed queen of spooky Halloween pranks." She gave Phil a sidelong glance, expecting him to protest. Stevie and Phil had a very competitive friendship, and it wasn't like him to let a challenge from Stevie pass without comment.

But Phil seemed distracted. He was digging around in his jacket pocket, looking worried. "Listen, you guys, I think I left my watch inside," he said. "I took it off during the meeting because the band was pinching me, and it must have fallen out of my pocket."

"Then it's probably still lying on the floor in the indoor ring," Lisa said.

Carole nodded. "You'd better go get it before a horse steps on it."

"Good point," Phil said. He glanced around at all three girls. "Want to walk me in? It must be about time for you to start tacking up."

Lisa glanced at her own watch. "Oops, you're right. We'll have to hurry if we don't want to be late."

Inside, the girls said good-bye to Phil, then hurried to the tack room.

"Maybe we should get together later and do some more planning," Lisa suggested as she slung a bridle over one shoulder. "We don't really have much time if everything's going to be ready by Saturday."

"Good idea," Carole agreed. "How about a Saddle Club meeting at my house right after our lesson?"

"It's a deal," Stevie and Lisa replied in one voice.

"I THINK MY father will let us use some of his old military uniforms," Carole said as The Saddle Club walked toward her house from the bus stop. A light rain was falling, but the girls were so busy discussing where they could find costumes for the city kids that they hardly noticed.

"Great," Stevie said. "They'll be too big, but that'll be part of the fun. I wonder if my brothers will let me borrow some of their sports team uniforms?"

"Probably not," Lisa predicted with a laugh. "But I'm sure they'll let you have their old Halloween costumes. Didn't you say something about pirates earlier?"

Stevie snorted. "Believe me, we have more pirate costumes than you can shake a peg leg at. Besides that, once in

14

a while they actually come up with something original. Alex was Paul Revere last year, and Chad went to a party as Rusty the Robot. He painted a bunch of cardboard boxes silver and wore them. But just as he was walking home from the party with some girl he had a crush on, it started to pour. Chad's boxes got a little soggy, and before he knew it they had fallen right off. He had to run home wearing only his long johns. The girl never spoke to him again." Stevie grinned. "My only regret is that I wasn't there to witness it."

The girls were still laughing when they walked into the Hansons' kitchen. Colonel Hanson was there pouring popcorn into the popper. "Hi, girls," he said when he saw them. "Your after-stable snack will be ready in a minute. In the meantime, why don't you towel off. Oh, and Stevie, your parents called a few minutes ago. They want you to give them a call right away."

"Uh-oh," Stevie muttered, heading for the phone. "I wonder what my brothers are blaming me for now."

Carole, Lisa, and Colonel Hanson laughed. They all knew that Stevie's brothers did their best to get Stevie in trouble with her parents as often as possible. But they also knew that Stevie's own mischievous nature was a lot more likely to get her in hot water than her brothers were.

While Stevie dialed her number, Carole and Lisa filled Colonel Hanson in on Saturday's event. Colonel Hanson nodded when Lisa mentioned the name of the organization.

"City Kids/Country Kids is a good group," he said. "I've

read about some of the work they've done in D.C. You girls should be proud of helping such a worthwhile cause."

"Funny you should mention helping, Dad," Carole said. "I was just about to ask if you'd like to come along and help on Saturday."

"I thought you'd never ask," Colonel Hanson exclaimed. "I'll be there with bells on."

"Actually, we were hoping you'd be there with your uniform on," Lisa said. "We're all supposed to come in costume."

"I see," Colonel Hanson said, rubbing his jaw thoughtfully. "And you thought I might like to dress up as, say, an officer of the United States Marine Corps?"

"Right," Carole replied.

Colonel Hanson gave both girls a smart salute. "Orders understood. You can count on me."

Just then Stevie, who was still on the phone, let out an excited shriek. "You're kidding!" she cried, almost dropping the receiver.

"What is it, Stevie?" Lisa asked.

Stevie waved a hand for quiet, her attention on her conversation. "When does she . . . that soon? How did she convince them to let her come? Uh-huh. Hmm. I see . . . Oh, that sounds like fun. Everyone here will be glad to see her. . . . Of course. Okay, thanks for telling me, Mom. I'll be home in time for dinner. Right now I've got to tell Lisa and Carole the news!"

She hung up and turned to her friends. "Dinah's coming!" she announced.

"Dinah?" Lisa repeated blankly.

But Carole understood right away. "She is? Oh, that's great!" she exclaimed. "Remember, Lisa, Dinah Slattery is the girl Stevie went to visit in Vermont that time. She used to live in Willow Creek, and she rode at Pine Hollow before you started going there."

"Oh, that's right," Lisa said. "She used to go to Fenton Hall with you, right, Stevie?" Stevie attended a private school called Fenton Hall, across town from the public school Carole and Lisa attended.

"I think I remember her," Colonel Hanson put in. "She's the one Stevie used to get into all kinds of trouble with."

"That's the one," Carole confirmed. Stevie just grinned.

"When is she coming?" Lisa asked.

"That's the best part. She's flying in Tuesday afternoon and staying until Sunday, so she'll be able to help with the Halloween event," Stevie said. "Her school in Vermont has a midsemester break, and her parents are going on a cruise for their anniversary at the same time. Naturally, she convinced them to let her come here for a visit."

"That's great," Carole said. "Don't you have a couple of days off from school, too?"

"Yep," Stevie said. "Thursday and Friday Fenton Hall is closed for teachers' meetings. Dinah will be able to come to school with me on Wednesday and see all her old friends.

Then we can spend all day Thursday and Friday at Pine Hollow."

Carole let out a mock groan. "Lucky you. Meanwhile Lisa and I will be slaving away at school. Still, I can't wait to see Dinah again."

"And I can't wait to meet her," Lisa added. "I've heard so much about her that I feel like I already know her."

"She feels the same way about you," Stevie assured her. "I bored her silly with stories about The Saddle Club when I was in Vermont. She knows all about you."

"And with Dinah here to help, I'm sure you girls will make this Halloween one those city kids will never forget," said Colonel Hanson.

"True," Stevie said. "Dinah's almost as good at coming up with fun stuff as I am." She glanced at Carole. "Remember the time she filled Veronica diAngelo's expensive new riding boots with cat food?"

Carole laughed. "I sure do. The locker room smelled like tuna for weeks. And I remember the look on Veronica's face when she found out who did it. I don't think she ever really forgave Dinah."

"It's a good thing Veronica is away on vacation with her parents until after Halloween, then," Lisa said. Veronica diAngelo, a spoiled, snobbish girl who rode at Pine Hollow, had just left with her wealthy parents for a two-week vacation in Italy.

"I guess so," Stevie said. "Although it would have been fun to team up with Dinah to torture Veronica, for old times' sake." She shrugged. "But with her gone we'll have more time to plan for the Halloween event—bugging Veronica is a full-time job. Maybe Dinah can help me play a few Halloween tricks on Phil instead."

The popcorn had finished popping. Colonel Hanson poured it into a bowl and salted it. "Here you go," he said, handing it to Carole. "Enjoy."

"Thanks, Dad," Carole said. She carried the bowl of popcorn into the living room. Her friends followed.

Stevie was still thinking about the good times she'd had with Dinah. "Most of our greatest triumphs took place at school, not the stable," she told the others. "There was the time Dinah had the idea to free all the crickets from the science lab. They used them to feed the snakes and frogs and stuff. The only problem was, we kind of lost control of them before we got their cage outside. There was chirping in the halls of Fenton Hall for months afterward."

Lisa laughed. "No wonder you and Dinah are such good friends," she told Stevie. "You sound like two of a kind."

"They sure are," Carole said. "Dinah was always a lot of fun at Pine Hollow. We were all sad when her family moved away." She took a pad of paper and a few pencils out of her father's desk, then sat down on the floor beside the popcorn bowl. "Come on, we'd better start planning. We've got the costumes to figure out, and don't forget the treasure hunt Max asked us to plan."

"Don't worry, I've got plenty of ideas for that," Stevie said.

"Me too," Lisa said. "But there's one thing I don't have any ideas for at all, and that's my own costume. Since we weren't planning to dress up this year, I hadn't thought about it at all."

"Me neither," said Stevie. "But I'm sure I'll come up with something before Saturday."

"It'll be hard to beat our costumes from last year," Carole said. "Remember? The three blind mice?"

"Hey, that gives me an idea," Lisa said excitedly. "Why not do a group costume again? Maybe we could be the Three Stooges."

Stevie shook her head. "That's a good idea, Lisa, but it won't work. Dinah will be here—there will be four of us, remember?"

"Well, then we could be the Four Horsemen of the Apocalypse," Carole joked. "After all, we'll be on horseback part of the time."

"The what?" Stevie repeated blankly.

"Oh, it's just this old movie my dad is always talking about," Carole said. "Anyway, I was just kidding. Actually I already have an idea for my costume."

"Really? What is it?" Lisa asked.

Carole shook her head and smiled. "You'll have to wait and see. It's a surprise. Besides, I'm not even sure I'll be able to do it."

"Well, if you think of any more brilliant ideas, let me know," Lisa said.

"If you're really desperate, I'm sure Alex would let you

borrow his Paul Revere costume," Stevie offered. "At least that has something to do with horses."

Lisa shrugged. "I don't know," she said. "I'll think about it. It doesn't really seem spooky or exciting enough for Halloween, though."

"Speaking of spooky and exciting," Stevie said, grabbing a handful of popcorn, "thinking about all those pranks Dinah and I used to play at school gave me an idea. Wouldn't it be great to play a Halloween prank on her while she's here?"

Carole laughed. "She'd probably love that. It would be just like old times." She glanced at Lisa. "Stevie and Dinah didn't just play practical jokes on other people—they were also constantly playing them on each other."

"Right," Stevie said. "But we were so good during my visit to Vermont that she'll be completely off guard and not expecting a thing. It's the perfect opportunity. It will be sort of a welcome-back-to-Willow-Creek prank." She sighed. "Now I just have to think of the perfect prank."

"Well, we'll try to help you come up with something if you promise us one thing in return," Carole said.

"What's that?"

"That you'll stop talking about Dinah's visit long enough to help us do some planning for Saturday," Carole replied with mock sternness.

Stevie laughed and agreed.

21

TUESDAY MORNING SEEMED to crawl by for Stevie. By the time she got to English class, she couldn't believe the day wasn't even half over. At least it was almost lunchtime. Then there would be only a few classes to go until her father picked her up on his way to the airport to meet Dinah's plane. Carole and Lisa were going, too.

Stevie couldn't wait. The only unfortunate thing was that she still hadn't been able to come up with just the right prank to play on Dinah. She had thought of idea after idea but rejected all of them. Either they were too obvious, they were too difficult to set up, or they'd been done before. Now, while the rest of the class was busy reading some boring short story in their textbooks, Stevie racked her brain. She thought about turning all Dinah's clothes inside out while she was sleeping, or giving her a mask with black ink on the inside, or trying to convince her that Pine Hollow had been bought by foreign investors, or telling her that Veronica diAngelo had joined The Saddle Club. She even thought about rigging something in Mr. Toll's wagon so that Dinah would fall out halfway through the hayride on Saturday.

That last idea was the silliest one yet, but it made Stevie think of something else. "I've got it!" she shouted suddenly, sitting bolt upright in her seat. When she realized where she was, she blushed and looked around at the surprised faces of her classmates.

"All right, Stevie," Ms. Milligan, the English teacher, said dryly. "You seem to have been particularly moved by this story. So I'm sure you won't mind answering a few questions about what we've just read."

"Uh—uh—" Stevie stammered, glancing down at the textbook page. The title at the top was "The Sisters' Day Out." That didn't sound too complicated. Stevie had faked her way out of more difficult problems.

"First of all, Stevie, what did you think was the major conflict in this story?" Ms. Milligan asked.

"Um, I guess it was the conflict, um, between the two sisters?" Stevie ventured.

The teacher looked a little confused. "Well, that's an odd way of putting it," she remarked. "What do you think the turning point of the story was?"

Stevie was feeling more confident now. "It was when they decided to go out," she said.

"When they decided to go out?" Ms. Milligan repeated. "Exactly when was that?"

"Um, after they talked about it?" Stevie said, once again uncertain. Maybe this wouldn't be as easy as she'd thought.

"Talked about it?" the teacher repeated again. "Stevie, you know I encourage interpretive readings in this class, but really—just who did you find doing any talking in this story?"

"Well, the sisters," Stevie said.

Ms. Milligan shook her head. "Stevie, you didn't read the story at all, did you?"

Stevie gulped. "I—I started to," she said. "But then I got distracted by, um, thinking about the title."

The teacher shook her head again, looking exasperated. "Well, I'll let it go this time, Stevie. But for future assignments," she added sternly, "please try to read a little farther than the title. Although honestly, even for pure guesswork, your answers have me mystified."

Stevie sank down into her seat, her face flaming. The teacher surveyed the room. "Jason, could you tell us what you thought was the main theme of the story 'The Two Birch Trees'?"

Stevie's gasp of surprise was drowned out by the ringing of the bell signaling the end of class. Sheepishly she flipped through her English book to the correct page and glanced down at the title of the story she was supposed to have been reading. "Who cares about a couple of stupid trees, any-way?" she muttered, slamming the book shut. "I've got more important things to think about." She grinned. One of those things was her new idea for a prank. She was sure it would work. It was so simple that it was perfect.

A few minutes later Stevie was seated at a table in the cafeteria with Patty Featherstone, Gail Porterfield, and Betsy Cavanaugh. All of them had known Dinah before she moved, and all of them were eager to see her during her visit to Fenton Hall the next day. And, of course, all of them remembered the practical jokes and other assorted trouble that had made Dinah and Stevie famous—or rather, infamous.

"Do you remember the time you and Dinah had Miss Fenton's high-school yearbook picture blown up to poster size?" Patty said as she dug into her plate of sliced turkey and lima beans.

"Yeah, and then they hung it on the front of the podium during morning assembly," Gail put in eagerly. "Poor Miss Fenton had no idea why everyone was laughing all through her speech about the canned-food drive."

"That was nothing," Betsy put in. "My favorite was the time Stevie and Dinah replaced all the ketchup in the cafe-teria with three-alarm hot sauce. That was pure genius."

"You only say that because you brought your lunch that day," Gail objected. "Some of us will never look at a ham-burger with ketchup the same way. No, if you want to talk genius, let's talk about the time they started that rumor that all classes would be taught in French instead of English."

"Please, please," Stevie said, waving a hand modestly. "You flatter me." But the more she heard her friends reminisce about her past triumphs, the more excited she got about Dinah's visit. "We did have some good times, didn't we?" she remarked.

"Sure," Betsy said. "But you got in an awful lot of trouble, too. Remember when you were having a mashed-potato-shooting contest and your spoonful missed the trash can—"

"—and hit Miss Fenton right in the ear," Gail finished with a giggle. "That was pretty funny."

"Hey, I never said I had perfect aim," Stevie said. She picked up a spoonful of lima beans and squinted at the nearest trash can. "Although I'm sure I have improved a little. . . ."

With that, she let the spoonful of beans fly. Unfortunately they missed the trash can—but not Ms. Milligan's ear. Stevie hadn't even noticed that her English teacher was walking toward the trash can until it was too late.

"Oops," she said, cowering down in her seat as the teacher, glowering, headed for her.

"So, Dad, as a lawyer, what do you think? Do I have a case?" Stevie said into the phone in the school office. She had just called her father at work to give him the news. Thanks to the lima bean incident, Ms. Milligan had ordered her to serve detention for an hour after school that day. "I mean, I tried to explain that I have an important errand to run after school today, but they refused to listen, even when I promised to make up the detention next week."

"Sorry, honey," Mr. Lake replied. Stevie wasn't sure, but she thought he sounded just a little bit as if he might be trying not to laugh. She didn't think that was very sympathetic of him. He knew how much she was looking forward to meeting Dinah at the airport. "I guess your friends and I will just have to go without you this afternoon. You can meet us at home."

"But Dad!" Stevie exclaimed. "Don't you think this qualifies as unfair imprisonment, or maybe cruel and unusual punishment? How about a writ of habeas corpus? Isn't that the kind of thing lawyers are supposed to do for their clients?"

"First of all, you're not my client—you're my daughter," Mr. Lake pointed out. "And secondly, have you ever heard the phrase 'if you do the crime, you've got to do the time'?"

"Thanks a lot, Dad," Stevie muttered. She sighed. "But if you happen to think of a legal loophole between now and three o'clock, let me know."

LATER THAT AFTERNOON Mr. Lake, Carole, and Lisa walked into the airport. "Let's see," Mr. Lake said, scanning the computer monitors listing incoming flights. "It looks as though Dinah's plane is due in about five minutes. The gate is this way. Come on."

The girls followed him across the terminal. "I still can

hardly believe it," Lisa said happily, returning to the conversation she and Carole had been having in the car.

"Now, what's all this excitement about?" Mr. Lake asked as the three of them sat down on some plastic chairs near the gate. "From what I gathered on the way here, something exciting happened at Pine Hollow yesterday, but I was too busy fighting traffic to catch what it was."

"Max asked Lisa to help give riding lessons to the city kids on Saturday," Carole said. Seeing that Mr. Lake still looked confused, she explained, "It's a real honor."

"A real honor for me, she means," Lisa added. "He asked Carole to help, too, but that's only natural—she's the best rider in our class."

"But the fact that he asked you means he thinks you're one of the best riders, too," Carole told her friend, giving her arm a squeeze. "And that's really something, considering you haven't been riding nearly as long as most of the other students. You should be proud of yourself."

"I guess I am," Lisa admitted, her eyes shining. "Oh, Max asked Stevie to help, too," she told Mr. Lake quickly. "He knows she's the best rider after Carole. But she can't do it because she's going to be busy setting up the treasure hunt."

"Hmm," Mr. Lake said. The girls had the feeling that he still had no idea what they were talking about. But they also had the feeling that he was used to that condition—after all, he lived with Stevie. "Well, anyway, congratulations seem to be in order, Lisa."

"Thanks," Lisa said. She leaned back in her chair and

smiled. "It's really going to be a pretty exciting week, isn't it? I mean, first this, and now Dinah's about to get here, and this weekend is Halloween."

"It really is," Carole agreed. "And look! That must be Dinah's plane!"

The girls and Mr. Lake stood up and watched as a sleek silver airliner slowly pulled up to the terminal. A few minutes later, passengers started pouring out.

"There she is," Carole shrieked. "Dinah! Dinah Slattery! Over here!"

Lisa saw a slender blond girl detach herself from the crowd and head toward them. A big grin lit up her face. A duffel bag was slung over her shoulder.

"Carole! Mr. Lake!" she cried. "I can't believe I'm really here! I didn't think I was going to survive the airline food."

Mr. Lake reached for her duffel and set it down next to the seats. "Don't tell me this is all the luggage you have," he said. "Did you check a suitcase?"

Dinah nodded. "They said the luggage should be out right away. Hey, where's Stevie?"

"It's a long, very Stevie-like story," Mr. Lake said. "Why don't you girls stay here and visit, and I'll go down to the baggage pickup area."

"Great! Thanks a lot," Dinah said. "It's a red leather suitcase with a blue strap around it. My name is on the tag."

"Got it. I'll be back in a jiffy," Mr. Lake said, hurrying toward the escalator.

"Dinah, this is Lisa Atwood," Carole said.

29

"Hi, Dinah," Lisa said politely, extending her hand. "I've heard so much about you from Stevie."

"Same here," Dinah said, glancing at Lisa's hand and then taking it. "Like, she said you had good manners, and I guess she was right."

Lisa blushed. She supposed it was a little formal to offer to shake hands, but the gesture had been automatic, thanks to years of training by her parents. "Um, well, anyway, welcome to Virginia—I mean, welcome back," she said lamely.

"Welcome back is right!" Dinah exclaimed, turning to Carole. "I can't believe I haven't been here at all since we moved. How are things at Pine Hollow? Still the same?"

"Always," Carole said with a giggle. "You know Max and his traditions."

"Well, actually there's a lot going on there right now," Lisa said, eager to share some of the exciting news with the visitor. "Did Stevie tell you about the Halloween party we're giving for some underprivileged kids on Saturday?"

"A little," Dinah said. "She said there are going to be a bunch of games and activities, like a hayride and a treasure hunt."

"And riding lessons for the kids," Carole added.

"That's right," Lisa said excitedly. "Carole and I are both going to help teach. We're the only students Max asked," she couldn't help adding, still feeling proud of her selection as assistant instructor.

"Well, Carole always was the teacher's pet as far as Max is

concerned," Dinah said, giving Carole a playful punch on the arm. "And I guess you must be one at Pine Hollow as well as at school, huh, Lisa?"

"What?" Lisa said.

"Oh, Stevie told me about you," Dinah said with a grin. "She said teachers and other adults just love you to death. She said your grades are always practically perfect—just like everything else you do."

Lisa frowned. She was pretty sure Dinah was joking, but she didn't want her to get the wrong idea before they'd even gotten to know each other. "Well, being a teacher's pet has got nothing to do with why I was picked for this," she said. "I worked hard to earn this, just like I do for my grades at school."

Dinah shrugged, looking a little taken aback. "Hey, I didn't mean anything bad by it," she said. "I was just repeating what Stevie said."

Lisa was sure Stevie might have said something like that, but she was equally sure it hadn't come across as an insult, the way Dinah made it sound. Taking a deep breath, Lisa decided a change of subject would do them all good. "Stevie said you've been taking riding lessons in Vermont, Dinah," she said. "How do you like your new stable?"

"Yes, how is it there?" Carole put in quickly. She was sensing some tension between Lisa and Dinah. She figured the best way to smooth things over would be to get the girls talking about a topic of mutual interest—namely, horses.

"Stevie told us about some of the horses there, and they sound wonderful."

Dinah laughed. "Carole, to you *all* horses sound wonderful," she pointed out.

Carole laughed, too, and agreed. "But seriously, how's your riding going? Is the instructor in Vermont as good as Max?"

"Oh, he's excellent," Dinah said. "I'm learning a lot from him."

"That's good. Having a good teacher really makes a difference, doesn't it?" Carole said. She'd thought about that a lot, since she was considering becoming a riding instructor someday—unless she decided to become a trainer, a breeder, a vet, or a competitive rider instead.

"It does," Lisa said. She was thinking about the task ahead of her on Saturday. She hoped she'd do well, and she hoped the kids would appreciate it. "Although I guess it helps to have good students, too."

Dinah glanced at Lisa. "Is that why you're already helping to teach?" she asked. "Because you're such a good student?"

Lisa shrugged. It wasn't what she had been thinking, but she supposed it was true. "I guess so," she said. "I've been working really hard to catch up to Carole and Stevie ever since I started riding—although I'm sure I won't really be able to catch them, since they've both been riding so much longer than I have."

"Just how long have you been riding?" Dinah asked, a bit sharply.

"She started about six months after you left, Dinah," Carole answered for Lisa.

"Well, I guess that disproves your theory about catching up then, Lisa," Dinah said with a little frown. "It sounds as though you've already caught up and passed me, and I've been riding almost as long as Stevie has."

"Well, that wasn't really what I meant . . . ," Lisa began, feeling awkward. Somehow she had managed to make Dinah feel bad about herself, and that wasn't what she had been trying to do at all, even if Dinah herself had been a little snooty with those comments about Lisa's being the teacher's pet. Still, Lisa was nothing if not polite—hadn't Dinah said so herself?

Meanwhile, Carole was searching her mind frantically for another topic. "Listen, Dinah," she said. "Stevie was just reminding us of some of the pranks you two used to pull. Do you have anything in mind for Halloween?"

Dinah's face brightened immediately. "Did you talk about the cat food incident?" she asked eagerly. "I'll bet Veronica is still steaming about that one."

"Oh, I don't know," Carole said with a laugh. "We've managed to distract her with a few good pranks since you left. Right, Lisa?"

"That's for sure," Lisa agreed.

"Well, I don't know," Dinah teased. "After all, you guys are just amateurs. When Stevie and I get together, though —now that's magic."

"I'm sure you'll have a chance to practice that magic

while you're here," Carole said. "I think Stevie has some ideas about playing some Halloween tricks on Phil."

"Oh, that's right!" Dinah exclaimed. "I'm finally going to get to meet the famous Phil! I can't wait. He sounds like a lot of fun."

"He is," Lisa said, making one more effort to be friendly. "He's a really great guy. He and Stevie are perfect for each other."

"It sounds like it," Dinah said. "Stevie said that even if everyone else around is being totally boring, she can always count on Phil to liven things up."

"Well, the rest of us aren't exactly boring . . . ," Lisa began, immediately on the defensive again. From everything Dinah was saying, she obviously thought Lisa was some kind of completely dull Goody Two-shoes. Lisa glanced over at Carole. To her surprise, Carole was smiling and nodding as if she agreed with everything Dinah had just said. She didn't seem to have noticed the insult at all.

"You know what I mean," Dinah said to Lisa with a shrug. "Stevie needs someone to challenge her once in a while. That's why she and I were always such good friends. And that's why it's so great that she has someone like Phil around now."

Before Lisa could come up with an answer to that one, Mr. Lake strode up, swinging a red suitcase. "Did I get the right one, Dinah?" he asked cheerfully, bending over to pick up Dinah's duffel bag.

"You sure did," Dinah told him. She reached toward the bags. "Here, I can carry one of those."

"Nonsense," Mr. Lake said firmly. "You're the guest. Now, tell me all the news. How are your parents?"

Dinah and Mr. Lake headed toward the parking lot, with Dinah laughing occasionally as Mr. Lake filled her in on why Stevie hadn't been able to come to the airport. Carole and Lisa followed silently, each of them thinking that this visit might not turn out to be as much fun as they had all thought it would be.

4

"DINAH!" STEVIE SHRIEKED, rushing out of the house, where she had been impatiently pacing the front hall ever since arriving home from school twenty minutes earlier.

"Here she is, Stevie, safe and sound," Mr. Lake announced, climbing out of the car and heading for the trunk to get Dinah's bags. "Even without your personal welcome at the airport."

But Stevie wasn't paying any attention at all to her father, and neither was Dinah. "I can't believe I'm really here," Dinah exclaimed happily. "I'm so glad I could talk my parents into this visit!"

"Of course you could," Stevie told her. "How could you not? I taught you everything you know."

Carole rolled her eyes at Lisa as the two of them got out of the car. "If that's true, we could be in for an interesting few days."

Lisa just nodded. She had hardly said a word on the ride home from the airport.

"Excuse me, but I think you got that backward," Dinah retorted with a grin. "I taught you everything *you* know. Remember when I showed you how to remove the tape of the national anthem from the school PA system?"

At that, Stevie and Dinah burst into uncontrollable giggles.

"What?" Carole demanded. "What happened?"

After a moment Stevie managed to stop laughing long enough to speak. "We replaced it with a tape of the school band playing 'Turkey in the Straw.'"

"Speaking of the school band," Dinah said as all four girls followed Mr. Lake into the house, "remember that Christmas concert when we were in fifth grade?"

"How could I forget?" Stevie said. "How could anyone forget? It was one of our finest moments."

"What happened?" Carole said again, thinking she sounded a little like a broken record but not really minding. She had forgotten how much energy and fun Dinah always brought to things—just like Stevie. Anyone would have fun when the two of them were around. Carole hoped that meant the awkwardness between Dinah and Lisa would pass once they got to know each other a little better. "What did you two do?"

"We convinced everyone in the band—we were both in it then, too—to play 'Jingle Bell Rock' instead of 'O Come All Ye Faithful' during the candlelight procession," Dinah said.

Stevie's eyes were sparkling. "The best part was that the choir was supposed to sing along, but we didn't tell them about the change," she added. "They caught on pretty quickly, though. Poor Mr. Sutter didn't know what hit him!"

Carole shook her head, smiling. "So what did he do to you when he figured it out?"

"We were very politely asked not to be in band anymore," Dinah said solemnly. Then she and Stevie burst into giggles again.

Mr. Lake reappeared from the kitchen. "Stevie, I've put Dinah's bags in your room," he reported. "Why don't you help Dinah make herself at home while I start dinner? Your mother and the boys should be home in a little while."

"Uh-oh, the terrible three," Dinah said, referring to Stevie's three brothers. "I can't wait to see them again, believe it or not." As the girls headed up the stairs toward Stevie's room, she added teasingly, "And I was just telling Carole and Lisa how I can't wait to meet the famous Phil."

"Well, you'll meet him, all right," Stevie said. "He's going to be helping at Pine Hollow on Halloween." She led the others into her bedroom. "Well, here it is," she announced to Dinah with a sweeping gesture.

Dinah glanced around and smirked. "As neat and tidy as

ever, huh, Stevie?" she said, taking in the cluttered piles of books, clothes, and who-knew-what-else strewn all over the floor. "I'm glad to see you cleaned up in honor of my visit."

Carole laughed. "You know Stevie," she said. Just then Carole noticed that Lisa was staring at the floor, still silent. Carole's smile turned to a frown. Her friend seemed extremely uncomfortable. Could it really be just because of the conversation at the airport? Lisa and Dinah hadn't exactly hit it off, but this seemed more serious than she'd realized. Something had to be done. Two wonderful people like Lisa and Dinah shouldn't be deprived of each other's friendship because of a few stupid misunderstandings.

Dinah wandered over to Stevie's dresser and peered at a framed photograph of Belle, Stevie's horse. "Is this her?" she asked excitedly. "She's beautiful! I can't wait to meet her in person. Or should I say, in horse?"

That gave Carole an idea. She glanced at her watch. "Maybe you shouldn't have to wait," she suggested. After all, if anything could bring Lisa and Dinah together, it was horses. Hadn't Carole just been thinking the other day that horses were almost always the perfect solution to any problem? "We should have time before dinner for a quick visit to Pine Hollow."

"What a great idea!" Stevie exclaimed. "And Dinah, there's another really special horse you have to meet besides Belle."

"I know," Dinah said, smiling at Carole. "Starlight, right? I've heard rave reviews of him."

"Well, him, too, of course," Stevie said. "But that's not who I was talking about. I meant Max's brand-new horse."

Carole furrowed her brow. As far as she knew, Max hadn't bought any horses lately. What was Stevie talking about? Before she could open her mouth to ask, she noticed Stevie winking wildly at her. Carole kept quiet. This new horse Stevie was talking about must have something to do with the prank Stevie wanted to play on Dinah.

"What brand-new horse?" Dinah asked.

Stevie let out an exaggerated sigh. "Oh, she's gorgeous!" she exclaimed dramatically. "She's probably the most beautiful horse I've ever seen in my life. She's a jet-black mare named Black Magic, and she's just the daintiest and prettiest thing you'll ever see."

Carole glanced over at Lisa with a tiny shrug. Lisa shrugged back, still looking glum.

"She's really athletic, too," Stevie continued. "She's great at dressage, plus she can jump higher fences than any of the other horses. Max is sure she could easily escape from any field he put her in if she wanted to, but luckily she's got a really sweet and friendly temperament, so she never tries."

"She sounds wonderful," Dinah said, looking excited. "I can't wait to meet her—and all the other new horses, too. And of course I can't wait to see all my old pals like Patch and Delilah." She frowned. "Didn't you tell me that Pepper died, Stevie?"

Stevie nodded, glancing at Lisa. Pepper had been Lisa's regular mount until his retirement. He had died the previous fall, and even though Lisa loved riding the sweet Thoroughbred mare Prancer, Stevie and Carole knew she still missed Pepper. They all did.

"That's too bad," Dinah said sadly. "I always kind of thought of Pepper as my horse."

Lisa gasped. "No he wasn't," she said before she could stop herself.

Dinah frowned. "What did you say?"

"Nothing," Lisa said quickly. "I was just saying that a lot of people thought of Pepper that way, not just you."

Dinah's frown deepened a little. "Well, that doesn't mean I can't be sad that he's gone," she said.

"We'd better get going before it's too late," Carole interrupted, her voice just a little too loud.

"Right," Stevie said eagerly, not noticing either Carole's anxious look or the other girls' angry ones. "After all, we don't want to keep Black Magic waiting—or any of the others, either."

The girls went downstairs just in time to greet Mrs. Lake and Stevie's brothers as they came in the front door. "Dinah!" Mrs. Lake exclaimed, putting down her briefcase and stepping forward to give the visitor a hug. "It's so good to see you again! How's your family?"

"She can tell you all about it later," Stevie said, tugging on her mother's sleeve. "We're going for a quick visit to Pine Hollow before dinner, okay?"

"Well, I suppose it's all right," Mrs. Lake said, taking off her coat. "Just don't be too long." She sniffed at the deli-

41

cious scents that were beginning to waft out of the kitchen. "It smells like your dad is making his famous Lake lasagna. You don't want to miss that."

While Dinah was trading playful insults with Stevie's brothers, Chad, Alex, and Michael, Carole pulled Stevie aside. "So what's the story with this imaginary Black Magic, Stevie?" she whispered. "What gives?"

Stevie grinned, with a sidelong glance at Dinah. "Just play along," she whispered back.

"OH, IT'S SO great to see all these familiar faces again!" Dinah exclaimed, rubbing Delilah's soft nose. The palomino snorted, as if agreeing, and all four girls laughed.

Out of the corner of her eye, Carole noticed that Lisa was looking a little more relaxed, and she smiled. Her friends might sometimes tease her about her belief that horses could solve almost any problem, but this time it seemed true.

"How about one more familiar face?" came a voice from behind them.

"Max!" Dinah exclaimed, rushing forward to give him a hug.

"Hi, Dinah," Max said, a little breathless from her enthusiasm. "Welcome back to Pine Hollow. I suppose you'll be here twenty-four hours a day for your whole visit, if your friends have anything to say about it."

"You'd better hope we're here practically that much,"

Stevie reminded him tartly. "If you're counting on us to make Saturday a success, that is."

"Touché," Max admitted with a smile. "Well, enjoy yourselves. And Dinah, don't forget to stop and say hello to my mother." Max's mother, known to all the young riders as Mrs. Reg, helped him run the stable. She was a kindhearted woman who was a favorite with everyone who knew her. "I think she's still around here somewhere." With a wave, Max hurried away.

"Come on, let's stop by Black Magic's stall, and then we'll go see Prancer," Stevie suggested. "That's the horse Lisa usually rides. After that we'll stop by Mrs. Reg's office."

"Great," Dinah said. "I was wondering when I was going to get to meet this perfect horse."

Carole and Lisa had been wondering the same thing. Now they followed as Stevie led Dinah down the aisle past Delilah, stopping in front of an empty stall.

"Oh, no," Stevie wailed. If Carole and Lisa hadn't known better, they would have thought their friend was experiencing the bitterest of disappointments. "She's not here!"

Dinah peered into the clean-swept stall. "A horse lives here?" she asked in disbelief.

Stevie shrugged. "Oh, you know Red," she said. "He's such a clean freak. I guess Black Magic must be out on the trail, and he's in the middle of giving her stall a good cleaning." Red O'Malley was Pine Hollow's head stable hand.

"Isn't it a little late for her to be out on the trail?" Dinah asked, looking worried. "It's getting pretty dark out there."

"Oh, I'm sure she'll be back soon," Stevie said. "Probably one of Max's adult riders wanted to take a moonlit ride through the fields or something." She moved briskly down the aisle. "Come on, you can meet Prancer instead. She's almost as pretty."

The gentle bay mare stretched out her head to greet the girls as they approached her stall. Lisa reached forward to give her an affectionate pat. "Here she is," she told Dinah. "Isn't she gorgeous?"

"Definitely," Dinah agreed sincerely. "She's a Thoroughbred, right?"

Lisa nodded. "She used to be a racehorse," she said. "That means she's a genuine blue blood. It's really exciting to have the chance to ride such a terrific horse."

"I'm sure it is," Dinah said, a little coldly. "I guess it's probably some kind of special honor Max only grants to his favorites."

Before Lisa could reply, Stevie jumped in. She was still thinking about her practical joke. "Nobody's bloodlines are as good as Black Magic's, though," she said. "She's really one of a kind. You don't need to look at her registration papers to tell how aristocratic she is."

Carole rolled her eyes. Stevie was really laying it on thick about this mystery horse. What was she trying to do? Whatever it was, Carole could tell it was distracting her so much that she still hadn't noticed the iciness between Lisa and Dinah.

44

"Come on," Carole said. "We'd better go see Mrs. Reg before she leaves for dinner or something."

The girls headed for Mrs. Reg's office, off the tack room. The woman recognized Dinah immediately and greeted her warmly. While the two of them chatted about Dinah's new home in Vermont, The Saddle Club wandered into the tack room and sat down to wait.

"Stevie, are you ever going to tell us what this Black Magic business is about?" Carole asked.

"It's my practical joke on Dinah," Stevie said with a grin. "I'm going to string her along, building up this incredible horse until she's simply dying to meet her."

"Then what?" Lisa asked.

Stevie smirked. "You'll see."

At that moment Mrs. Reg and Dinah walked into the tack room, still talking. "I really miss this place, you know," Dinah said, running her hand over a gleaming saddle. "But I'm glad to see that everything is just the way I left it." She peered into the bucket in a corner of the room where the saddle soap was kept. "Make that almost everything," she added.

"What do you mean?" Stevie asked.

Dinah grinned. "Well, either you've found a new place to keep the saddle soap, or Max and Mrs. Reg aren't keeping the place up to their usual standards. This bucket is empty."

Mrs. Reg frowned, and for a second the girls thought it was because of Dinah's playful insult. But when she peered into the bucket, the frown deepened into a worried scowl. "That's odd," she muttered. "Very odd indeed."

"What is it, Mrs. Reg?" Carole asked.

The woman looked up, as if just remembering that the girls were in the room. "Oh, nothing," she said, a little too quickly.

Stevie wasn't buying that. "Come on, Mrs. Reg," she urged. "What gives?"

Mrs. Reg sighed wearily. "I refilled that bucket to the rim with fresh bars of saddle soap just this morning."

"Someone must have cleaned an awful lot of tack, then," Lisa said, glancing down at the large, empty bucket.

"I don't think so. And that's not the first weird thing that's happened around here lately," Mrs. Reg said, shaking her head slowly. She sat down on the edge of a trunk, looking thoughtful. "Did you girls ever hear of Nevermore Stables?"

All four girls shook their heads.

"It was in the next county, but it closed before any of you were born," Mrs. Reg said. "It *had* to close."

"Why?" asked Dinah.

"Well, some folks say it was because there weren't enough students in the area to pay the bills," Mrs. Reg replied. "But then again, some say it was something else. That the students were scared away."

"What do you mean, scared away?" Carole asked skeptically. "How do you scare someone away from a stable?"

Mrs. Reg didn't answer Carole's question. Instead she

asked one of her own. "Have you girls ever heard of poltergeists?"

"Sure," Lisa said promptly. "They're a sort of mischievous, playful ghost."

"Not always so playful," Mrs. Reg corrected. "They can be very destructive, if you believe the people who say they've been haunted by them. Like the people at Nevermore. After almost a year of mysterious, annoying, sometimes dangerous mishaps—misplaced tack, unlatched gates, odd tapping and banging noises, things like that—they had no choice but to close down. The students were convinced it was a poltergeist at work, and they quit in droves."

"But that's ridiculous," Carole said. "Even the best-run stable has an occasional accident."

Mrs. Reg glanced down at the bucket, and the worried crease in her forehead deepened. "Occasional, yes," she said softly. "But when the occasional becomes the everyday, well . . ."

Stevie laughed. "Mrs. Reg, you're not seriously suggesting that a poltergeist is haunting Pine Hollow, stealing all our saddle soap!"

"Of course not," Mrs. Reg snapped. Without another word, she got up and stalked back into her office, closing the door firmly behind her.

The four girls traded bewildered glances. "What was that all about?" Dinah exclaimed. "I mean, I remember Mrs. Reg's stories are always a little out there, but really. Soap-stealing ghosts? That's a wild one, even for her!"

"No kidding," Carole said. "But as usual, I have no idea what she was actually trying to tell us. I doubt it was that Pine Hollow is haunted." Mrs. Reg's stories usually had a moral, but her listeners often had to work hard to figure out what it was.

Carole glanced at her watch. "Oops!" she said. "I'd better go call my dad and tell him to pick me up here. It's navy bean soup night at the base, and he hates to be late for that."

"Oh, rats," Stevie said, looking disappointed. "I was going to invite you guys to have dinner at my house tonight in honor of Dinah's first night. You heard my mom—it's Lake lasagna tonight."

"Sorry," Carole said regretfully. "But you know how my dad feels about navy bean soup."

"How about you, Lisa?" Stevie said. "You'll come, won't you?"

Lisa stared at her fingernails, trying not to meet Stevie's eye. "Um, I can't," she mumbled. "I promised my parents I'd eat at home tonight."

"Well, just call them," Stevie suggested. "I'm sure they'll let you come when you tell them why."

"No, I don't think so," Lisa said.

Stevie's eyes narrowed, and she glanced from Lisa to Dinah and back again. It finally dawned on her that the two of them hadn't been acting particularly friendly. In fact, they had barely spoken to each other at all. She bit her lip. How could she not have noticed before now? And more importantly, how could two of her best friends in the world not be friends themselves? She decided they just needed a little more time to get to know each other. Working together on the Halloween event was sure to do the trick.

"All right, then," Stevie said to Dinah. "It's just you and me, kid. And the rest of my family, of course. Speaking of which, we'd better get going, or my brothers will eat everything in the house before we get back."

The two of them hurried away. Carole knocked gingerly on Mrs. Reg's door, but there was no answer. "I guess I'll have to use the pay phone. Do you have a quarter?" she asked Lisa.

Lisa dug a handful of coins out of the pocket of her jeans. "Here's one," she said.

The two girls walked to the pay phone in the corridor. "My dad can drop you off if you want," Carole offered. "Your house is right on the way to the base."

Lisa nodded. After Carole had finished her call, the girls headed outside to wait for Colonel Hanson. It was dark and chilly, and there was a hint of dampness in the air.

Carole wrapped her arms around herself. "It sure feels like fall, doesn't it?" she remarked.

Instead of answering, Lisa said, "I don't think Dinah likes me."

"I don't know about that," Carole said. "But I definitely got the impression that you don't like her."

Lisa looked a little surprised. "I'm trying to like her," she said. "I really am. After all, she's one of Stevie's best friends. There's no reason I shouldn't like her."

"But?" Carole prompted.

"But I guess we don't have much in common," Lisa said, scuffing her feet through a pile of orange and yellow leaves. "We're completely different from each other."

"Just like you're completely different from Stevie, and Stevie's completely different from me, and I'm completely different from you," Carole reminded her. "That's part of what makes The Saddle Club so great, remember? Not just what we have in common, but what we don't."

"I know," Lisa said. "You're right." She shrugged. "I don't know what it is with Dinah. I was all ready to love her, especially after everything you guys said. But she just rubs me the wrong way or something."

"Well, if you can't get over it, maybe you should just try to stay out of her way while she's here," Carole advised. "She's only visiting for a few days, and we're all going to be pretty busy."

"I guess so," Lisa said. But she wasn't completely satisfied with that solution. Even when Dinah was back in Vermont, she would still be Stevie's friend, and Carole's, too. And Lisa would still be the odd one out. Even if the others didn't think of it that way, she knew in her own mind she always would. And what would that mean for The Saddle Club?

WHEN STEVIE AND Dinah arrived at Pine Hollow after school the following afternoon, they found Carole and Lisa already hard at work. There were no more riding lessons scheduled for that day, so they had taken over the room where the students' lockers were, turning it into an impromptu arts-and-crafts room.

"Look at this," Carole exclaimed when Stevie and Dinah walked in. She held up a neatly lettered sign proclaiming COSTUMES. "Lisa did it—doesn't it look nice? We're going to put it on the costume box."

"It looks great," Stevie agreed. "What are you working on now?" She peered over Lisa's shoulder at the notebook she was busy writing in.

"First we made up a schedule for the day," Lisa said.

"That way we knew how much time to allow for each activity." She flipped back a page in the notebook and pointed at the chart she'd made. "Now we're starting to plan what we'll need for the treasure hunt."

"Aha!" Stevie exclaimed, grabbing a pen from the floor. "Pass the notebook. This is my specialty. Come on, Dinah, I'm sure we can come up with some fun stuff for the kids to find."

Lisa handed her the notebook. "I started a list on this page," she explained. "I put down the name of the object, how many we'd need, and where we can get them."

"Uh-huh," Stevie said, glancing at the list.

"Let's start our list on a new page," Dinah suggested. "We'll just list all the fun and crazy things we can think of, and worry about those other details later."

"Okay," Stevie said agreeably, flipping to a clean page. "I've got one. Monster masks. My brothers have a million of them, and they'll be perfect for Halloween. We can plant them all through the woods on branches and stuff."

Lisa bit her lip. She couldn't believe Stevie and Dinah were just starting over, ignoring the careful system she and Carole had worked out. She glanced at Carole to see how she was taking it.

"How about stirrups?" Carole suggested. "I'm sure Max would let us use some—and we should have at least a few horsey objects. And since they're silver-colored, they'll really seem like treasure."

"Great idea!" Dinah said, scribbling it down. "And we

ought to have something the kids will really want to find, like candy. Maybe lollipops."

Lisa sighed. Obviously she was the only one bothered by Stevie and Dinah's disorganization. "I'll be right back," she said quickly, escaping from the room and heading for the bathroom. She wanted to let off some steam, and she wanted to do it in private. It was clear that she was the only one who had a problem with Dinah, and she had resolved to follow Carole's advice and keep it hidden from her friends. There was no sense in spoiling their visit just because she was unhappy.

A few minutes later Lisa felt calmer. She returned to the locker room to find that Phil had arrived. She greeted him and sat down next to Carole, who was making name tags for the Pine Hollow people. Lisa took the one with Red O'Malley's name on it and started sketching a spooky ghost on it.

Dinah was asking Phil about Black Magic. She was disappointed that the mare was out on the trail again—she was dying to meet her.

Phil nodded seriously. "She's one great horse, all right," he said. "I've never seen anything like her." Lisa took that to mean that Stevie had called him and let him in on the joke. She almost felt sorry for Dinah. The girl seemed so eager to see the wonderful horse everyone kept talking about, she was sure to be disappointed when she found out it didn't exist, not to mention embarrassed that she'd been taken in by Stevie's prank.

A few minutes later the talk turned from horses to costumes. Phil described the magician's outfit he had put together, then turned to Dinah. "What are you going to be?" he asked.

"I'm going as Paul Revere," she replied. "Stevie offered me her brother's old costume, and I guess it's better than cutting a couple of eyeholes in an old sheet like I was planning."

Lisa's eyes widened, and she dropped the marker she was holding. Paul Revere? But Stevie had already offered that costume to Lisa! Lisa had decided not to take it—she had come up with a better idea the day before. But she hadn't had a chance to tell Stevie that yet.

"I hope you don't mind, Lisa," Stevie said offhandedly, as if guessing what her friend was thinking. "You didn't seem too excited about it, and Dinah really needed something to wear."

Lisa clenched her teeth. "Of course not, Stevie," she replied carefully. "Anyway, I need to have a costume I can ride in, for when I help Max with the lessons. That's more important than dressing up, you know." As soon as the words left her mouth, she realized they sounded a little mean. Dinah was sure to know that Lisa was thinking that her own role in Saturday's events was much more important than Dinah's, especially since it was obvious to all of them that Lisa could ride just as easily in a Paul Revere costume as in anything else.

Dinah frowned, and there was a moment of awkward

silence. Finally Phil cleared his throat. "You know, Dinah, I was just thinking," he said. "I could really use an assistant for my act. I'd ask Stevie, but she's already volunteered to set up this treasure hunt instead. And besides, I don't want to give away the tricks of the trade to just anybody. How about it? Do you want the job?"

Dinah's eyes lit up and she grinned at him. "Hey, that sounds like fun," she exclaimed. "I've always loved magic shows. Now I'll get to be in one!"

Stevie stuck out her tongue at Phil, but then she smiled at him. Lisa knew Stevie was grateful to Phil for making Dinah feel included. Then Stevie turned and gave Lisa a surprised look, as if wondering what had gotten into her. Lisa didn't meet her friend's eye.

"Say, Stevie, speaking of my magic show," Phil said. "I've been looking all over for a red stable blanket to use in my act. Do you think Max has any?"

Stevie shrugged. "There are probably some in the tack room," she said. "In that big trunk against the far wall."

Phil gave her a sheepish look. "Would you mind looking?" he pleaded. "I can never find a thing in that tack room."

Stevie rolled her eyes and got up. "Yeah, sure," she said skeptically. "If that's your excuse for being lazy, who am I to question it?" She headed for the door.

STEVIE WALKED SLOWLY toward the tack room, deep in thought. The scene between Lisa and Dinah had upset her, and she needed time to think things through. For one thing, she could tell that Lisa was upset about the Paul Revere costume. Stevie had been sure Lisa hadn't wanted to wear it, otherwise she would never have offered it to Dinah. She had expected Lisa to know that.

She sighed. The night before, Dinah hadn't said much about her first impression of Lisa, and that was a bad sign. Dinah and Stevie had discussed practically every other person and horse they knew at great length. But by mutual, unspoken agreement, Lisa Atwood's name had barely come up. Stevie didn't like that one bit. She was crazy about Lisa and Dinah, and she knew they could be great friends if they both tried a little harder. But she wasn't sure how to tell either of them that without making them mad at her, too.

Finally Stevie reached the tack room. "Hmm, that's funny," she muttered to herself. "I wonder why the door is closed?"

Pulling open the door, she stepped forward into the darkened tack room . . . and felt something move against her leg.

She let out a piercing shriek, stumbled backward, and fumbled for the light switch. When the bulb came on, Stevie went limp with relief and started to laugh.

She was still laughing when her friends arrived seconds later, brought running by her scream. Stevie could only gesture into the room. The others looked and saw that it was flooded in a sea of black cats. They were perched on the saddle racks, climbing in and out of trunks and buckets, and generally milling around and getting into things.

"What's going on in here?" Carole gasped. "Where did all these cats come from?"

Stevie stooped down and reached for a small black kitten with a white spot on its nose. "Let's see—this is Regret, and right next to her is Big Ben." It was a Pine Hollow tradition to name all the stable cats after famous horses. "And over there, I recognize Merganser and Idle Dice and Scamper—"

"Why would someone put all these cats in here?" Lisa interrupted.

"All these *black* cats," Dinah pointed out. "It must be

57

some kind of pre-Halloween prank. A pretty funny one, too."

"Maybe it was that poltergeist Mrs. Reg was talking about," Carole joked.

"No, I don't think so," Stevie said, narrowing her eyes at Phil and stroking Regret's head. Phil just shrugged. Stevie glanced around. "The only one missing is Snowball," she commented, referring to Carole's own black cat. She clucked her tongue. "Come on, kitties! Back to work. You have mice to catch, you know." With her friends' help, she shooed most of the cats out of the tack room.

"Back to work for us, too?" Carole asked.

"I don't think so," Stevie said. "Dinah and I have to get home. My parents are taking us into Washington for dinner."

"Lucky you," Phil said. "You can tell who has the rest of the week off from school. Before you go, maybe Dinah and I should plan our practice schedule for the show."

"Okay," Stevie said. "While you do that, the rest of us will clean up in the locker room." Lisa and Carole followed Stevie as she hurried down the hall, dodging cats at every step.

"Boy, who would have guessed the mall would be so crowded?" Stevie complained as she and Dinah walked into the stable the next afternoon. The two girls had spent the morning shopping for costume parts and other Halloween props for Saturday.

"I guess everyone wanted to get out of the rain," Dinah said, shaking the water out of her hair.

"Well, I think every parent in Willow Creek with a preschool-age kid must have been there," Stevie said. "If I hadn't gotten in line at the pizza place while you were finishing up at the bookstore we would have starved to death."

Max rounded the corner at that moment and saw the two girls standing there. "What's this? Two sets of idle hands?" he demanded.

"We just got here, Max." Stevie held up the shopping bag she was holding. "And we got lots of great stuff for the party!"

"That's nice," Max replied. "But while you're doing all this party planning, don't forget we have horses to take care of. For instance, I just noticed some pretty dirty stalls that could use cleaning . . ."

"We can take a hint, Max," Dinah said with a laugh. "We'll get right to it." She handed Stevie another shopping bag. "But first I'm going to the bathroom. I'll be back in a sec."

"Okay," Stevie said. Humming to herself, she carried both bags into the locker room and dropped them on a bench. Then she took off her jacket, shook most of the rain off it, and shoved it into her locker.

While she waited for Dinah, she dug through the bags of goodies from the mall, pleased with their purchases. They had decided that the treasure hunt should have three categories of hidden objects: monster masks for Halloween, gold and silver for tradition, and lollipops for fun. The girls had taken care of the last category at the mall, buying a huge bag of multicolored lollipops. They had also found a few inexpensive gold and silver objects at the dime store, such as a big, gold-colored plastic crown. Stevie couldn't wait to start hiding the objects, but she knew she'd have to. If she left any of them in the woods for too long before the kids started searching, raccoons and other animals would be sure to make off with them. She would have to hide most of the treasure on Saturday morning.

"I'm back," Dinah announced, walking into the locker area. "And I had a great idea. Before we get to work, why don't you finally introduce me to Black Magic? I'm sure she can't be out on the trail today—not in all this rain."

Stevie gulped, her mind racing. "Uh, she's not here today," she said. She's, um, on the—I mean, at the farrier's, being fitted for special shoes."

"She's at the farrier's?" Dinah repeated. "But shouldn't the farrier come here?"

"Not for this kind of shoe," Stevie explained. These shoes have to be specially fitted with a special kind of machine, so the horse has to go there to have it done. She won't be back until Saturday morning." Stevie could hardly believe Dinah was buying the ridiculous story, but she didn't seem suspicious at all. "It's all the rage these days here in Virginia," Stevie added helpfully.

"Oh, well," Dinah said sadly. "I hope I get to see her sometime before I leave."

"I'm sure you will," Stevie assured her. "Now, come on. There are some pitchforks out there with our names on them!" She hurried out into the aisle before Dinah had a chance to respond—or to think any more about Black Magic's high-tech shoes.

Rounding the corner toward the tack room, Stevie stopped short. Dinah almost ran into her. "What's wrong?" she asked.

"Someone left a chair in the aisle," Stevie replied. Sure enough, there in the aisle in front of the tack room was one of the folding chairs from Mrs. Reg's office. Sitting on it was a paperback book. Stevie stepped forward and picked it up. *"Poltergeists: The Mischievous Menace,"* she read aloud. "It's a book about poltergeists!"

"Really?" Dinah hurried over and grabbed the book from Stevie. She paged through it, pausing to examine some of the photographs inside. "Wow! Check this out." She held up the book to show Stevie. "Look, it has pictures and everything. It says the word 'poltergeist' is a German term that means a noisy ghost that flings things around. And there's a whole list of examples of places that were haunted by poltergeists. Pretty spooky."

"There's only one spooky prankster around this stable," Stevie declared. "And his name is Phil Marsten." She dragged the folding chair down the hall and shoved it back into Mrs. Reg's office.

"But Stevie, how could Phil have done this?" Dinah asked, handing the book to her. "He left at the same time we did last night. If he'd sneaked away to set this up we would have seen him. And besides, you know as well as I do that Max and Red would never let this chair sit around in an aisle all night."

Stevie shrugged. "I don't know how he did it, but I'm sure he did," she declared. She walked back to the locker room and tossed the poltergeist book onto one of the benches. "Still, maybe I'll take that book home. We can read it to get ideas for tricks to play on Phil."

Dinah shrugged. "Well, if Phil was behind this, I'll have to admit I'm impressed," she said dubiously. "I sure can't figure out how he could have done it—not without skipping school, anyway." Like Carole and Lisa's school, Phil's was in session that day.

"Oh, he did it all right," Stevie said. "He did the other pranks that have happened around here, too—the missing saddle soap and the black cats in the tack room. And I'll figure out how, just you wait and see."

WHEN PHIL WALKED in with Lisa a few hours later, Stevie didn't say a thing about the chair and the book. She just smiled sweetly. "Hi, Phil. Hi, Lisa. How was school?" she asked.

"Fine," Phil replied. He set down his school backpack and pulled out a black vinyl bag with the words "The Magnificent Marsteno" lettered on the side. "But I'm sure you two had more fun here."

"That's for sure," Lisa agreed. "My math teacher gave us a pop quiz. I think half the class failed. I'm just glad I did a little studying last night after dinner."

"I'm sure you did well," Stevie said. "You always do. And without anything like the escaped-bull story, right, Dinah?"

Dinah giggled. "That was a good one," she said.

"What?" Phil asked. "Is this another story about some terrible prank you guys pulled in school?"

"It sure is," Stevie confirmed. She gave Phil a sidelong glance. "I'm sure you'll like this story—after all, you do have some experience with pranks yourself."

"This was a great one," Dinah said eagerly before Phil could respond. "Mrs. Tatnall decided to give us a pop quiz in science class one Monday, and nobody was prepared for it— especially not me and Stevie."

"That's right," Stevie put in. "We had spent the entire day before here at Pine Hollow and hadn't even thought about homework."

"So just as Mrs. Tatnall was passing out the test papers, Stevie suddenly jumped out of her chair and started yelling that she'd seen a bull escape from the field across the street."

"That was before they built the new post office there," Stevie explained. "There was just a huge field with some cows and a big, mean bull in it. Luckily the bull was no-where in sight at that particular moment, so I just explained that I could have sworn I saw him taking off across the street and heading around the corner of the school toward the playground."

"Mrs. Tatnall panicked and ran out to tell the principal to bring in the first-graders from recess," Dinah said. "She spent the rest of the class with the other teachers searching for the escaped bull. They kept looking until they finally noticed him coming over the hill—safely *inside* the fence."

"Later, I just told them that the shape I'd seen might have been the school janitor on his tractor. But better safe than sorry, right?" Stevie finished with a grin.

"Especially since we never did have to take that quiz," Dinah added. She glanced at Lisa. "Some people might like studying and taking tests, but not us—right, Stevie?"

Stevie glanced at Lisa. Dinah's remark had obviously been aimed at her, and Stevie was surprised. It wasn't like Dinah to be purposely mean. It seemed that she and Lisa were bringing out the worst in each other, and Stevie couldn't think of a thing to do to help. "Say, Lisa, where's Carole?" she said quickly instead of answering Dinah's question. "I thought she would come over with you."

"She couldn't," Lisa replied. "She has a dentist's appointment today, remember?"

"Oh, that's right," Stevie said. "Well, I guess we'd all better get to work then, since we're one hand short. Max already made Dinah and me do all the chores in the entire stable, so the rest of the afternoon is free for party preparations."

"Great," Phil said. He picked up his black bag. "Then my assistant and I can do some rehearsing. Okay, Dinah?"

"I'm ready when you are, O Magnificent Marsteno," Dinah said. "Where should we practice?"

Phil glanced at Stevie and Lisa and raised an eyebrow. "We'd better find a top-secret location," he said. "Far away from prying eyes."

Stevie snorted. "As if Lisa and I care about your silly little magical secrets," she said, waving a hand dismissively as the pair headed out of the room. "We have much more important things to do, thank you very much."

After they had gone, she turned to Lisa. "Now. What kinds of important things do we have to do?" she asked.

"First of all, we'd better finish those name tags we started yesterday," Lisa said, pulling the materials out of her locker. She was glad Dinah had gone off with Phil. It would be nice to spend some time with Stevie without the other girl around.

The two friends got to work. Stevie began lettering names onto the tags, copying from the list Max had given them. After she finished each one, Lisa drew a picture on the name tag and then attached a safety pin.

"I didn't want to say anything when Phil was in the room, but we had another visit from the Pine Hollow poltergeist today," Stevie said.

"Really?" Lisa asked, concentrating on the bat she was drawing. "What happened?"

"Someone—as if we couldn't guess who—stuck a chair in

the aisle near the tack room," Stevie said. "This book about poltergeists was on it. Subtle, huh?" Stevie got up and looked around the room. "Hmm. That's odd," she muttered.

"What?" Lisa asked, looking up.

"The book," Stevie replied. "It's gone." She shrugged. "Oh well. Maybe Dinah has it." She looked around once more, then shrugged again. "That must be it," she murmured. "She must have picked it up and moved it when I wasn't looking. Or maybe Phil stole it back."

"So you still think Phil is responsible for the weird things that have been happening around here?" Lisa asked.

"Of course," Stevie replied a little impatiently. "Who else could it be?"

"I don't know," Lisa said. "But it seems like some of these pranks would be hard for Phil to have done. I mean, what about that first thing, the saddle soap that disappeared on Tuesday. He wasn't even at Pine Hollow that day."

"So what's the explanation?" Stevie asked. "Do you really think a poltergeist is behind everything?"

"Of course not," Lisa said. "I'm just saying that most of it could have been coincidence. Maybe Mrs. Reg didn't put as much soap in that bucket as she thought she did. Maybe those cats chased a mouse into the tack room . . ."

"Only the black cats?" Stevie said skeptically. "And then who shut the door—the mouse? No, I don't think so. Besides, that book turning up in the aisle was definitely no coincidence. Somebody put it there, and I'm sure that somebody was Phil. And I'm going to prove it." With that, she settled down to work.

A few minutes later, Lisa peered over Stevie's shoulder at the list. "How many more names do we have to do?"

"After the one I'm doing now, about half a dozen," Stevie replied.

Lisa stood up and stretched. "Well, we're running low on safety pins," she said. "I'd better go see if Mrs. Reg has any." She wandered out of the locker room and down the hall toward Mrs. Reg's office. As she got closer, she heard giggles coming from the tack room. She glanced in as she walked past, then froze. Phil and Dinah were inside, their heads close together, talking and laughing. Phil's magic bag was lying near the door, unopened.

At that second Phil looked up and met Lisa's eyes. He stopped talking immediately and jumped to his feet awkwardly. "Oh—um—hi, Lisa," he stammered. "I didn't know you were standing there."

Dinah stood up too. Her face was beet red. "We were just —um—talking about the show," she said. "You know, practicing."

"Okay," Lisa said, backing away from the doorway. "Sorry I interrupted." She hurried into Mrs. Reg's office. No one was there, but Lisa spotted a small basket full of paper clips and safety pins on the desk. She grabbed a few of the pins, quickly scribbled Mrs. Reg a note telling her what she'd taken, and left. She didn't look into the tack room as she hurried past.

\*       \*       \*

". . . So THEN PHIL looked really embarrassed and said something about not seeing me standing there," Lisa told Carole over the phone. Lisa had called as soon as she arrived home from Pine Hollow. She hadn't said a word to Stevie about what she had seen in the tack room. She hadn't known what to say. But Lisa figured that if anybody could offer a sound second opinion on the situation, it was Carole.

"And then what?" Carole asked.

"Then Dinah said they were practicing, and then I left," Lisa said.

Carole sighed. "And that's all? So what?"

"So it just seemed really weird," Lisa said. "It was like I was catching them doing something—I don't know—*wrong.*"

"What are you suggesting, Lisa?" Carole asked, sounding mystified.

Lisa took a deep breath. She really wasn't sure herself. "I don't know," she said. "I just got the feeling that they wished I hadn't seen them right then. Like maybe they were doing something they wouldn't want Stevie to find out about."

"Oh, come on, Lisa," Carole said with a laugh. "I know you don't like Dinah very much, but if you're suggesting what I think you're suggesting—that she and Phil are having some kind of secret romance behind Stevie's back—

you're just plain crazy. Neither of them would ever do something like that."

"How can you be so sure?" Lisa asked, a little stung by Carole's words.

"I just am," Carole replied firmly. "And you can be, too, believe me. Just because you and Dinah don't get along, that doesn't make her a bad person."

"I know what I saw," Lisa objected. "And whether I like Dinah or not, I know there was something weird going on."

"Just forget about it, Lisa," Carole said. "They were probably just afraid you'd overheard one of Phil's precious trade secrets, that's all. Anything else you thought you saw was your own imagination working overtime. Maybe you've been reading too many of those teen magazine articles about cheating boyfriends or something."

Lisa bit her lip. When Carole put it that way, her suspicions did seem a little silly. After all, no matter how Lisa felt about Dinah, she knew that Phil was a good person and that he really cared about Stevie. "Maybe you're right," she said reluctantly.

"Of course I am," Carole said. "Don't worry. Dinah will only be here for a couple more days. You'll have to put up with her at my house tomorrow night and at Pine Hollow on Saturday, and then she'll go back to Vermont and things will get back to normal."

"Back to normal," Lisa repeated slowly. She wished she could believe it.

ON FRIDAY EVENING Stevie, Dinah, Lisa, and Carole were gathered in the Hansons' living room for a sleepover. Bright and early the next morning Colonel Hanson was going to drive them all to Pine Hollow to set up for the Halloween event.

"That was a terrific dinner, Colonel Hanson," Dinah said, rubbing her stomach as Carole's father walked into the room, dishtowel in hand. "Thanks for inviting us."

"Carole's friends are always welcome to our food," he replied. "Including our popcorn. How about it?"

Stevie groaned dramatically. "I don't know if I can eat another bite."

"Me neither," Carole said. "Especially since you won't even let us work it off by helping you with the dishes."

"Come on, you want to keep your strength up for tomorrow, don't you?" Colonel Hanson said. "I know you girls worked hard all week getting ready. Besides, if you're going to watch all these movies I rented for you, you'll need popcorn, right? I'll make a big batch as soon as I finish the dishes." He hurried out of the room before the girls could reply.

Stevie picked up the rented videos. *"The Blob, The Creature from the Black Lagoon*, and *Poltergeist,"* she read aloud. "Your dad is really in the Halloween spirit." She stifled a yawn. "I just hope they're good and scary. Otherwise I might not make it through all of them."

"There's one thing I don't understand, though," Carole said. "Usually at this time of year Dad insists that the old horror movies are the scariest ones. He refuses to watch anything made past 1959. So why would he rent *Poltergeist?* That's much more recent than the others."

"Did you ask him?" Lisa asked.

Carole nodded. "He just said it looked like something we would like," she said. "I guess it's because I've been telling him about the Pine Hollow poltergeist."

"Well, then, let's watch that one first," Stevie suggested. She got up and rummaged through her backpack as Carole put the videotape into the machine. Finally Stevie found what she was looking for. "That reminds me," she said, holding up a book. "I found that book I was telling you about, Lisa. It was in my locker today."

Dinah furrowed her brow. "In your locker?" she repeated.

71

"How did it get in there? I thought you left it on the bench."

"I did," Stevie said. "I thought you might have moved it."

Dinah shook her head. "I didn't even see it again after we found it yesterday."

"Well, maybe Max put it there," Stevie said uncertainly.

"Do you think Max was the one who knocked down all those hats today, too?" Lisa asked. Carole and Lisa had arrived at Pine Hollow after school, and the four girls had decided to go on a quick trail ride before finishing their party planning. When they returned, they found that the poltergeist had struck yet again. The hard hats, which were kept on hooks on the wall of the student locker room, had all been knocked to the ground.

"I guess not," Stevie admitted. "That's definitely not Max's style."

"And it couldn't have been Phil this time, either," Lisa pointed out. "He wasn't even there today. And the hats were fine when we left on our ride."

Stevie sighed. "All right, all right, I'm finally convinced that Phil couldn't be behind all these pranks," she said. She flipped through the pages of the poltergeist book. "I just wish I could figure out who is." She stopped to read something in the book. Her eyes widened. "Hey, listen to this, you guys. 'In most recorded cases, there has been at least one young person—usually a girl or young woman—living in the building haunted by the poltergeist.'"

"Weird," Carole said. "That sure seems to fit Pine Hollow. There are lots of young women and girls there, and according to Max, most of us *do* practically live there." She yawned. "But I still don't believe there's a poltergeist haunting the stable."

Stevie shrugged. "I don't either," she said. But her friends thought she sounded a little less certain than she had before. This close to Halloween, almost anything seemed possible.

"Come on, let's start the movie," Dinah suggested. She poked Stevie, who was still engrossed in the book. "Put that away. We should turn off the lights so the movie will be scarier."

Stevie tossed the book in the general direction of her bag, and the girls settled back to watch the movie. After a while Carole got up. "Give a yell if something scary happens," she said. "I'm just going to give Dad a hand with the popcorn."

When she returned a few minutes later, a warm bowl of salty popcorn in her hands, the first sight she saw on the television screen was a terrifying ghostly specter reaching out to threaten a little blond girl. She watched for a moment, chills running down her spine. Then, when the scene changed, she turned back toward the darkened room. "Hey, you guys," she complained. "I thought I told you to call me if something scary happened." She waited for a second, but there wasn't a sound from the other girls. "Guys?" A soft snore was the only reply. Carole switched on a lamp. All three of her friends were sound asleep.

\*     \*     \*

SATURDAY MORNING DAWNED overcast, damp, and breezy. "Perfect Halloween weather," Stevie announced as the four girls stepped outside and headed for the Hansons' station wagon.

"I hope you're right," Lisa said, casting an anxious glance at the gray sky. "It would be a shame if it rained today."

"Let's think positively," Carole suggested.

"Good idea," Dinah agreed. "Besides, it wouldn't dare rain after all the hard work we've done. Stevie's right—it's perfect Halloween weather."

"Everybody ready?" Colonel Hanson asked, joining them by the car.

"You look great, Dad!" Carole exclaimed. Her father was wearing his full dress uniform. His brass was gleaming, his shoes were polished to a shine, and every crease was perfect.

"Thanks, sweetheart," Colonel Hanson replied. "Now everybody into the car. We'd better hustle. You've got a lot to do before the kids arrive."

Phil was standing in the driveway when the station wagon reached Pine Hollow. "Finally!" he exclaimed as the girls and Colonel Hanson piled out of the car. "I thought you'd never get here. I've been waiting for at least ten minutes."

"Well, don't panic," Stevie told him. "We're here now."

Colonel Hanson headed for the stable entrance. "I'm going to see what Max needs help with," he said. "I assume you kids already know what you're supposed to be doing."

"We sure do," Stevie said as Colonel Hanson disappeared inside. She turned and started to follow him. "Let's get started."

"Wait a minute," Dinah put in. "Before we do, I have one request. Can I finally get to meet Black Magic now? You said she'd be back today from the farrier's."

"Oh." Stevie stopped in her tracks. She had been so busy planning the day's event that she'd all but forgotten about her prank on Dinah. She thought fast. "Actually, Dinah, I forgot to tell you," she said apologetically. "Max told me yesterday that he was sending her to stay at another stable for the day."

"He is?" Dinah wailed. "But why?"

"He didn't want her to become overexcited," Stevie said. "He thought the kids might be too noisy for her. She's very high-strung."

"Really? But I thought you said she had a sweet, friendly temperament," Dinah said. "You said she never tried to escape because she was so calm and nice."

"Oh," Stevie said. "Yeah, I did. She's really sweet and nice as long as there's not too much noise. That's the one thing she can't stand." She shrugged. "You know how horses can be."

"Sure," Dinah replied. "I'm just disappointed, that's all. After everything you've told me, I'm dying to meet her. Do you think I'll get to see her before I leave tomorrow?"

"Oh, I'm sure of it," Stevie said.

"Come on, then," Phil said. "We'd better get to work. By

the way, Stevie, Max said to tell you that it's okay to use some of the stirrups from the blue trunk for your treasure hunt."

"Great," Stevie said. "I'm going to go get them."

"We'll come with you," Carole said, glancing at Lisa. "We should probably look over the ponies' tack and make sure it's ready for the riding lessons."

"Okay," Phil said. "While you're doing that, Dinah and I have some last-minute rehearsing to do. We'll meet up with you again in a little while."

The two groups headed their separate ways. "I can't believe it," Carole said as soon as Phil and Dinah were out of earshot.

"What?" Lisa asked.

"That Dinah hasn't caught on to this whole Black Magic business yet," Carole said. "I mean, Stevie hasn't exactly been convincing."

"Hey, what do you mean by that?" Stevie asked, pretending to be hurt.

Carole rolled her eyes. "Come on. That shoeing story was ridiculous. And why on earth would Max send one of the horses away just because some kids are coming? They see kids every day."

Stevie shrugged. "It is pretty amazing that she doesn't suspect anything," she admitted as they turned the corner toward the tack room. "But it does tie in perfectly with my master plan."

"Which is what?" Lisa asked.

But just then Stevie let out a gasp. "Look!" she exclaimed. The girls had just reached the doorway of the tack room. Inside, everything was in its usual disordered state of order—except for one thing. Every bridle in the room was hung upside down on its peg.

"Who could have done this?" Carole asked in amazement. "This must have taken forever!"

"Maybe a poltergeist with a lot of time on its hands?" Lisa suggested weakly.

Stevie shook her head. "This is really getting weird," she commented. She patted her backpack. "I'm glad I brought that poltergeist book with me today. I'm beginning to think I may need it." Her friends weren't sure if she was joking or not. They decided not to ask.

None of the girls had much time to think about ghosts, real or otherwise, for the next few hours. There was a lot to be done before the city kids arrived at one o'clock. While the other Pony Clubbers were hard at work preparing for the kids' barbecue dinner and hanging decorations around the stable, Stevie was kept busy gathering a few last-minute props for the treasure hunt. Dinah and Phil had disappeared to one of their secret rehearsal places to make their final preparations. Carole and Lisa had to check over the ponies' tack, and then the ponies themselves, for the riding lessons. Besides all that, of course, there were still the everyday chores to be done.

"Oh, there you are," a harried-looking Red O'Malley said, peering into the tack room, where Carole and Lisa were busy polishing the ponies' saddles one more time. "Listen, could one of you do me a big favor? All this activity is getting to Prancer a little, and she's kicking at her stall. . . ."

"Say no more," Lisa said. "I'll go try to calm her down." It was well known at Pine Hollow that Prancer preferred young riders to adults. Lisa knew that she would have a much better chance of calming the mare than Red would.

"Thanks, Lisa," Red said gratefully.

As Lisa hurried down the aisle toward Prancer's stall, she could understand why the mare was upset. Even by Pine Hollow's usual busy standards, the stable was awfully noisy today. Most of the horses were unperturbed—the hustle and bustle was no different from the atmosphere before a horse show or gymkhana. But Prancer was still young, and she hadn't been at Pine Hollow as long as most of the others. Lisa knew that with time and experience the mare would learn to settle down. She smiled at the thought that Prancer was having the same problem Stevie had claimed the fictional Black Magic was having.

"I know it's a little noisy today, girl, but don't be alarmed," she murmured softly to the horse, reaching over the half door of her stall. Prancer's ears swiveled toward her, and Lisa could have sworn the mare was listening carefully —and understanding every word. She knew that Max would scoff at that idea. But that didn't mean it wasn't true. "It's a pretty exciting day for all of us," she continued. "But it's good-exciting, not bad-exciting. I guess it's hard for you to tell that, though; to you, it just seems like a lot of scary extra noise."

Beneath the riot of other sounds, Lisa heard a softer one much closer by. She stopped talking to the horse and listened, still automatically rubbing Prancer's velvety muzzle. Lisa frowned. The noise seemed to be coming from an unoccupied stall just across the aisle, and it sounded like whispering and giggling.

"I'll be back in a second, Prancer," Lisa whispered to the mare. Prancer just blinked calmly in response and stepped over to her feed bin. Lisa's familiar presence had settled her down already.

Lisa tiptoed across the aisle, still listening intently. She flattened herself against the door of the stall next to the one the sounds were coming from. The voices were a little louder now.

"Oh, come on, Phil!" exclaimed one of them. It was Dinah's voice.

"No, I'm serious," Phil's voice came in return. Then he laughed softly. "Anyway, I'm sure she has no idea. Now come on, we'd better get out there before someone gets suspicious."

Lisa's eyes widened. Whatever they were talking about, it didn't sound like magic—black, white, or otherwise. And it didn't sound like good news to Lisa. She quickly backed away from the stall and tiptoed back across the aisle. Seeing that Prancer was now munching placidly at her feed bin, Lisa gave her a quick pat and hurried away around the corner of the U-shaped stall area. She didn't want Phil and Dinah to know she'd caught them once again. And she also didn't want anyone else to know this time. She wasn't ready for another lecture from Carole.

Lisa paused when she was a safe distance away and leaned against the wall, wondering what to do. If Dinah and Phil really were up to no good behind Stevie's back, wasn't it Lisa's duty as a friend to tell Stevie about it? She wasn't sure. And the worst part of it was, she wasn't sure Stevie would believe her even if she did tell her. It was just her word against Dinah's. Lisa knew that Stevie trusted her, but she seemed to trust Dinah, too, and she'd known her a lot longer than she'd known Lisa.

A snort from the stall behind her interrupted Lisa's thoughts. A second later, a soft nose pushed at her head. Lisa turned around and couldn't help smiling in spite of her dark thoughts. "Hi, Belle," she said, patting the friendly mare. "How's it going?"

Belle snorted again and backed away. Lisa peered into the stall after her and caught a glimpse of an unfamiliar gleaming object in the feed bin. Lisa sighed and unlatched the stall door. "Looks like our friendly neighborhood poltergeist has been at it again," she muttered, taking the cordless phone out of Belle's feed bin and heading down the hall to return it to Mrs. Reg's office.

8

"I'M NOT SURE she's ready for this," Lisa said worriedly, stopping in front of Prancer's stall and looking in. "She seems fine now, but I'm afraid that having a lot of strange kids around might spook her again."

Carole nodded, reaching out to stroke Prancer's smooth neck as the mare came over to greet them. "I don't blame you for being worried," she said. "Prancer is still very young, and these kids aren't used to being around horses. They could spook her and not even realize they're doing it. It wouldn't be safe for them or for her."

"I know." Lisa sighed. "I'd really love to ride her today—I'd really love to ride her just about any day of the year—but I think this time I'd better not."

"Don't worry," Carole said with a smile, giving Lisa a friendly squeeze on the arm. "She'll be here for you to ride tomorrow." She could sympathize with her friend's disappointment. Carole hated to be deprived of riding Starlight for even one day. He was relatively young and inexperienced, too, but thanks to Carole's hard work with him she was confident he was up to the task ahead. But she couldn't say the same about Prancer, and she knew that Lisa was making the right decision.

"I guess I'll go ask Max which horse I should ride instead," Lisa said. "Then we can tack up so the horses will be ready when it's time to start."

"Tell you what," Carole said. "I'll ask Max for you and then tack up both horses. That way you can get the costume box ready. I think that's the last thing we have to do before the kids get here."

"It's a deal," Lisa said. "Thanks."

"No problem," Carole said. "That's what friends are for, right?" She hurried away in search of Max.

Half an hour later, Lisa stepped back and admired her handiwork. She had just finished taping the sign she'd made onto the large cardboard costume box, which was sitting in the middle of the locker room. "Okay, I think that's everything," she said to Stevie, Phil, and Dinah, who were watching her. "We're ready for them."

Carole walked in and announced that Starlight and Barq were tacked up. She looked at her watch. It was almost one o'clock. The Saddle Club, Dinah, Phil, and all the others had been working furiously all morning, stopping only long enough to wolf down the sandwiches Max's wife, Deborah, brought them for lunch. But finally everything was done. The stable was sparkling clean and neat as a pin, except for the spooky Halloween decorations Meg Durham and Adam Levine had hung everywhere. The costume box was ready. Treasure stuffed in two large shopping bags stood waiting for Stevie to scatter throughout the woods. And two of Pine Hollow's ponies were groomed to perfection and stood in their stalls waiting to be tacked up for the riding lessons. Everything was ready.

"We still have one more thing to do, you know," Carole reminded the others.

"What?" Stevie asked.

Carole grinned. "Our costumes." She leaned over and grabbed a brown paper shopping bag out of her locker. "I'll be right back."

"When did she get so modest?" Stevie wondered as Carole disappeared in the direction of the bathroom.

"This must be the big surprise costume she's been so mysterious about," Lisa said. She opened her locker and grabbed the duffel bag that held her own costume.

"I left my magician costume in Mrs. Reg's office this morning," Phil said. "I'd better go get it." He left the room.

Stevie sat down on the bench in front of her locker and reached down to open the door. "I wonder what Carole . . ." Her voice trailed off.

"What's wrong, Stevie?" Lisa asked.

"The poltergeist has been at it again," Stevie replied, pointing.

Lisa and Dinah hurried over to look. Stevie's locker was packed full of currycombs.

"This is really weird," Stevie said. She took the currycombs out of the locker one by one, piling them on the bench next to her. "I just looked in here half an hour ago. I had that poltergeist book in my back pocket and it was getting in the way, so I stuck it in here. And the only things in the locker then were the book and my costume. Well, and my spare breeches, and my low boots, and half an apple, and a few other things . . ."

"We get the picture, Stevie," Dinah said. "The question is, who could have done this? Everybody has been in and out of this room a million times today. Anybody who tried to do this would have been caught for sure."

"Anybody human, you mean," Lisa said darkly.

"Surprise!" Carole cried at that moment, rushing back into the room.

Stevie gasped. "Carole! You're a jockey!"

Carole grinned and twirled around so they could see the whole costume. She was dressed in genuine blue-and-white jockey silks, complete with a cap, goggles, and a riding crop. "What do you think? I borrowed the whole outfit from Stephen, Mr. McLeod's jockey." Mr. McLeod was the owner of a local Thoroughbred racing stable. Max had bought Prancer from him.

"It's an amazing costume," Lisa said, and she meant it. Carole looked perfect.

"And the most amazing thing is that the clothes fit perfectly," Stevie said. "It makes you realize just how small jockeys have to be."

"I know," Carole said. "I was worried the pants would be too big and I wouldn't be able to ride in them. But they're just my size."

"Everybody ready?" Max shouted from the corridor outside. "The kids should be here any minute."

"Oops!" Dinah said. "We'd better get dressed too." She began pulling on the Paul Revere costume she had borrowed from Stevie's brother.

Lisa tried not to watch. She was still annoyed that Stevie had given away the costume without asking her. Lisa had decided to be a cowgirl. She was going to wear jeans and a Western hat.

Stevie finally got all the currycombs out of her locker and reached for her costume, which was wedged behind them. She had decided to dress as Betsy Ross—partly because it would go with Dinah's costume and partly because her mother had a reproduction of a Revolutionary War flag that she had reluctantly agreed to let Stevie use.

"What's with the currycombs?" Carole asked.

"Take a guess," Stevie replied, unfolding the flag and hanging it over a bench. "Our friendly neighborhood poltergeist has struck again."

"It does seem to be picking on you, Stevie," Carole said.

"I know," Stevie replied. She quickly pulled on her long colonial dress and tied a bonnet over her hair. "I think I'll take a quick look at that book. I don't remember reading whether they like to single out one young person to bother, or if they just pick on everyone as long as there's a young person around." She rummaged around in the bottom of the locker for a moment, then sat back on her heels with a frown. "That's funny," she muttered.

"What's wrong?" Lisa asked.

"The book," Stevie said. "It's not here."

Before the others could answer, Mrs. Reg stuck her head into the room. "Come on, girls," she said. "The bus just pulled into the drive. Let's get out front and welcome the kids."

All talk of poltergeists was forgotten immediately. The girls straightened their costumes and hurried out to the head of the driveway. There they met Phil and the other Horse Wise members.

"This is going to be fun," Meg Durham exclaimed, yanking at the skirt of her witch costume. "I love Halloween."

The others agreed. They watched as the bus pulled to a stop in front of the stable and a harried-looking young man disembarked and went to speak to Max. On the bus, elementary-school-age kids were peeking out the windows, looking excited.

A moment later the young man returned to the bus, and a second after that the kids began pouring off. For a while, pandemonium reigned. There were only a dozen city kids, but from the noise they were making there could have been twice that number. The boys and girls, all of them between the ages of six and ten, were obviously restless after their long ride from Washington. As soon as their feet touched the ground they started running around excitedly looking at everything—the stable building, the horse van, the outdoor ring, even the mailbox—shouting and shrieking the whole time. Susan Connors, the woman who had spoken to Horse Wise the week before, got off the bus with the kids. Despite her best efforts and those of the young man, the kids were completely out of control.

But before things could get really out of hand, Colonel Hanson stepped forward and raised his hand. "Atten-*shun!*" he shouted at the top of his lungs in his most official-sounding military voice. Instantly all the kids fell silent and turned to stare at him, wide-eyed.

"Whoa!" said one little boy with large dark eyes and long lashes. "He's like a real soldier or something!"

Max flashed Colonel Hanson a grateful smile and then turned away to confer with Susan Connors and the van driver about what time they should return for the kids.

Colonel Hanson stepped toward the boy who had spoken and saluted. "That's Colonel Hanson of the United States Marine Corps to you," he barked. "What's your name, private?"

"I'm Joe," replied the boy, returning the salute as best he could. "My uncle used to be a Marine too. But now he's a policeman."

Carole giggled. "He's adorable!" she whispered to Lisa.

Within minutes Colonel Hanson had found out all the kids' names and introduced them to everyone from Pine Hollow. Then, with true military precision, he had them line up in front of Max. "Mr. Regnery is the commanding officer around here," he told them sternly. "You listen to him."

A little girl named Lulu raised her hand timidly. "When do we get to see the horses?" she asked.

Max laughed and tossed Colonel Hanson a rather sloppy salute. "I think that's my cue to take over, Colonel."

Colonel Hanson smiled and saluted back. "Yes, sir!" He stepped back to join Carole and her friends.

"Now, to answer your question, young lady," Max said to Lulu. "You're going to get to see some horses right now. Is everyone ready to learn how to ride?"

There was a chorus of excited yells from the kids.

"I think they're saying yes," Stevie commented to her friends.

Max nodded to Carole and Lisa, who stepped forward. "First of all," he said, "we're going to break up into two groups, and then you'll get to see how we get horses ready for riding. It's called 'tacking up.'"

The group moved over to the outdoor ring, where the ponies were contentedly nibbling at some hay. "I think it's time for me to head for the woods," Stevie told Dinah and Phil as Max began dividing the kids into two groups. "Belle and I have got to plant the stuff for the treasure hunt."

"We'd better go finish setting up," Phil said. Dinah nodded. The three friends hurried off on their respective errands.

When Stevie arrived at Belle's stall, she stopped short. "Oh no, not again," she muttered. She stooped to pick up the poltergeist book, which was leaning against Belle's stall door.

Meanwhile, Red and Carole were leading one of the groups of kids toward a small paddock nearby that would serve as a second ring. Carole greeted the small gray pony inside with a pat on the neck. "This is Nickel," she told the kids. She gestured to the saddle and bridle that were waiting, draped over the fence. "In a minute I'm going to show you how to tack him up. But first, Red is going to go over a few very important rules that you have to remember when you're around horses."

Red nodded and cleared his throat. "Thanks, Carole," he said. "First of all, as you can see, horses are big, strong animals—even a relatively small one like Nickel, here. The horses here are very well trained and under normal conditions are gentle and obedient. But you have to remember that a sudden movement or a loud noise could frighten them, and then they can be dangerous. You always have to be aware of your horse's mood. One way you can do that is by watching his ears." He pointed at Nickel's ears, which were relaxed but alert. "You can see that Nickel's ears are perked forward. That shows that he's paying attention and isn't nervous or scared. If he were, his ears would most likely be flattened back against his head."

Red continued to discuss horse safety for a few more minutes, then turned and nodded to Carole. She stepped forward. "Now that we know a little about our horse and his moods, we're ready to start tacking up," she said. She clipped Nickel's lead line to the gate, then picked up the saddle and showed it to the kids. "We'll put the saddle on first. That'll give it time to warm up and settle while we put the bridle on."

She demonstrated how to position the saddle and the pad underneath it, sliding them back from the withers to be sure the pony's hair underneath was lying flat and smooth. Then she fastened the girth.

Red handed her the bridle. "First, we take off the halter —that's what this thing he's wearing is called," Carole explained. She quickly removed the halter and pulled the bridle on, sliding the bit into the pony's mouth and gently pulling the headstall over his ears. She adjusted the brow band and fastened the throatlatch and noseband, explaining what she was doing at each step.

"There," she said, giving the pony a pat. "Now all we have to do is double-check that girth. Sometimes when you tighten it, the pony holds his breath. Then when he lets his breath out the girth is too loose! After you check it again, you're ready to go."

"But first Carole is going to go get her horse," Red said. "She'll be showing you how to mount him."

90

"You have your very own horse?" asked a little girl in awe.

Carole nodded, thinking how lucky she was. It wasn't the first time she'd thought that, but looking at these kids, most of whom couldn't keep a puppy, let alone a horse, made her feel even more fortunate. "His name is Starlight," she said quietly. "I'll be right back."

Inside the stable door, she almost collided with Lisa. "How's it going so far?" Lisa asked.

"Great," Carole said. "How about your group?"

"Oh, they're wonderful," Lisa said with a smile. "That little boy Joe is a real character. He can hardly stop talking about his uncle the policeman. It turns out he's a mounted officer in Washington. He even taught Joe a little bit about riding."

"That's great," Carole said. "It's nice to know that even in the city there are still horses around."

"Of course there are," Lisa reminded her. "Don't you remember when we went riding in Central Park in New York City? And my parents once took me to watch a polo match on the Mall in Washington. There are horses everywhere!"

Carole grinned. "And that's the way it should be. But right now, we'd better get a move on so there will be horses out *there*!"

Lisa couldn't argue with that. Both girls hurried off.

A short while later, after demonstrating mounting, dismounting, and proper riding posture on Barq, Lisa watched as Max helped one of the kids onto Penny's back. She knew the lessons were going well, and she could tell that the kids were enjoying themselves. That was important to Lisa. Although riding was a lot of work in some ways, it was also a lot of fun. It occurred to her that this was probably a once-in-a-lifetime experience for most of the kids. That made her sad, but in her opinion once in a lifetime was at least a little better than never.

Lisa stepped forward to take Penny's lead and keep the pony still while Max helped the first rider find the stirrups. Max smiled gratefully at Lisa for knowing exactly what to do. She smiled back proud of herself for doing so well as assistant instructor. It was clear that Max was proud of her, too, and that made Lisa feel even better. The only thing she would have changed if possible was the horse she was riding during the lesson. She loved Barq, but she missed Prancer. Still, she knew that it was for the best. The mare would learn and improve with time, just as Lisa herself had. Right now Prancer just wasn't ready for this kind of situation.

The rest of the hour flew by. Each of the visitors had a chance to ride one of the ponies at a walk and a trot. Before Lisa knew it, it was time to put Nickel and Penny away and start the treasure hunt. Stevie had returned from hiding the objects, so that meant everything was ready. Lisa dismounted and watched as Adam Levine led the two ponies inside for a well-deserved grooming. She noticed that Adam had some carrots stuffed in his back pocket for the ponies, who'd been good as gold during the lesson.

"Do you want me to take Barq for you, Lisa?" asked Phil. He and Dinah had appeared a few minutes earlier to watch the end of the lesson. Lisa figured that meant the two of them were finished with their magic practice—or whatever else they had been doing.

"That's okay, Phil," Red said, overhearing the offer. "I'm going to take care of Starlight, and I can take Barq too. I think Max needs you guys to help out with the treasure hunt."

He was right. Max and Mrs. Reg were already breaking the city kids into groups of three. "We'll have four teams. Each team will have a name and a leader," Max announced. "You'll have one hour to find the things Stevie has hidden in the woods. The 'treasure' could be candy or anything gold or silver. That means stirrups, coins, whatever. And there are also a few Halloween surprises that I think you'll recognize. The team that finds and brings back the most treasure will be declared the winners and will have first choice of costumes."

The kids cheered. "I'm going to win!" Joe called out excitedly. "I want to be a pirate!" He swung an imaginary sword.

Max smiled at the little boy's enthusiasm. Then he turned to the older kids. "I'll need four leaders," he said. He looked at Carole first. "Carole, you can be the leader of the first group—the Ghosts. Phil, why don't you take the Ghouls, there." He pointed to Meg Durham and Betsy Cavanaugh. "Meg, you can lead the Witches, since you're already dressed for it, and Betsy can take the Goblins." He glanced at the sky, which still looked gray and threatening. "It looks as though it could pour at any moment," he added. "So leaders, be sure to stay close to home, and come straight back if it starts to rain."

"Be careful in the woods," Mrs. Reg warned the kids. "And listen to your leaders." She turned to Max. "I think it might help to have one or two people out there on horse-back, just to keep an eye on things and make sure nobody gets lost. Sort of a horseback lookout."

"Good idea," Max agreed.

"I'll do it," Stevie offered eagerly.

Max shook his head. "No way, Stevie," he said with a smile. "You've got to stay here and be ready to declare the winner. You're supposed to be in charge of this thing, after all." He turned to Lisa, who was leaning on the paddock fence beside Dinah. "Lisa, why don't you saddle up Prancer and do it?"

Lisa smiled and nodded. She was happy about the assignment for two reasons. First, it showed that Max thought she was capable and reliable. And second, it meant she would get to ride Prancer today after all.

But before Lisa could move, Mrs. Reg spoke up again. "Now Max, just because it's a special day I don't think we should ignore our rule about riding alone in the woods," she said. "Maybe Dinah should saddle up, too. She and Lisa can work as a team."

Max nodded again. "Dinah, you can take Nero. He's a

good, steady trail horse. He'll be a good match with Prancer."

Dinah and Lisa traded annoyed looks. Lisa could tell that Dinah wasn't any happier about the pairing than she was. But she knew it was no good arguing with Max once his mind was made up. They would just have to make the best of it.

9

"COME ON, EVERYONE!" Carole called out. "Let the treasure hunt begin!"

"And may the best team win," added Meg, giving a witchy cackle. With that, the four teams headed off across the fields while Lisa and Dinah hurried inside to tack up.

"I'll help you, Dinah," Stevie offered. "Nero is groomed and everything, so all we have to do is throw some tack on him and you'll be set."

Moments later Prancer and Nero were ready. Lisa could feel her mood darkening to match the cloud-heavy sky. The last thing she wanted to do was go riding through the woods alone with Dinah. They only had to spend one more day together; why couldn't they spend it at opposite ends of the stable, instead of side by side on the trail?

The two girls didn't exchange a single word all the way out of the stable yard and across the pasture. When they reached the trail leading into the woods, they heard excited young voices ahead of them. A moment later they caught up to Phil's group, which included Joe, the little boy who had been in Lisa's riding group.

"Hi, Lisa!" he called as soon as he spotted her, waving frantically and running toward her.

Lisa tightened her reins as she felt Prancer tense beneath her. "Be careful, Joe," she called to the little boy, trying to keep her voice calm and steady so that it wouldn't upset the mare any further. "Walk, don't run. Remember what Max and I told you during the riding lesson? You don't want to scare the horses with sudden movements."

Joe immediately stopped in his tracks, a contrite look on his face. "Sorry about that," he said. "I guess I forgot."

"Come on, guys," Phil said to Joe and the other two children in his group. "Let's stand off the trail and let the horses pass. We don't want to slow them down."

"Can't they walk with us for a while?" pleaded a little girl named Maria who had been in Carole's riding group. "The horses are so pretty."

Lisa looked at Phil and shrugged. "The trail's pretty wide here," she said. "I guess we could stick with you for a few minutes."

The little group ambled along through the woods. Lisa and Dinah made sure to keep their horses a safe distance behind Phil and the kids. It wasn't easy, though; while the other two kids kept themselves busy scanning the trail and nearby woods for the treasure, Joe was more eager to talk to the riders about his own riding experiences with his uncle.

Lisa was glad of the distraction. It meant that she and Dinah were kept so busy responding to Joe's endless stream of comments and questions that they barely had to speak to each other. *Maybe this ride won't be so bad after all*, Lisa thought.

And then disaster struck.

Joe was telling the riders a particularly exciting—though perhaps not entirely true—story about helping his uncle catch some dangerous criminals. ". . . and then we snuck up on them," he explained, crouching down and tiptoeing to demonstrate. "When we got close enough to their hiding place, we peeked in the window. And then my uncle jumped up, and *bang!*" Joe leaped into the air and shouted the last word, pretending to whip out a pistol.

That was too much for Prancer. At the sudden noise and motion, she stopped short, reared up, and whirled around. Lisa barely managed to stay aboard as Prancer let out a series of wild bucks and kicks, snorting all the time. Lisa did her best to regain control of the horse. Just when she thought she was beginning to get through to Prancer, a loud clanking echoed through the woods. Dinah had been backing Nero away, out of range of Prancer's flying legs, and one of the gelding's metal shoes had landed heavily on a large rock beside the trail.

That was all the panicked Prancer could take. She reared

once more, leaped off the trail, and set off through the woods at a dead run.

Lisa leaned forward, clinging to the mare's mane for dear life. She kept her head down and her arms in as sharp branches reached out and ripped at her hair, clothes, and skin. It took all the riding skill she had to stay in the saddle at all. If she were to fall now, she could be very seriously injured, but she barely thought about that because she was too busy worrying about Prancer. The mare's racing career had ended because she had a weak pedal bone, which had been injured in her last race. It had healed perfectly, but Lisa knew that the weakness was still there. If Prancer took a wrong step now and injured the leg more seriously, it could cost the mare her ability to walk—or even her life.

Finally, after what seemed like an eternity, Lisa could sense that the mare's frantic wild pace was slowing. Either Prancer had recovered from her panic or she was tiring—probably both. Lisa sat up a little and looked around. Prancer's wild ride had taken them straight through a thick, overgrown part of the forest, far from any of the trails Lisa knew.

"Oh, Prancer," she said as the mare finally slowed to a canter, then a trot. "Where have you taken us?"

Finally regaining control, Lisa brought Prancer to a stop in the middle of a clearing, then slid off. She calmed Prancer with her hands and voice for a few minutes. When she was sure the mare was perfectly calm, she checked her carefully for injury, paying particular attention to Prancer's weak leg. Aside from some nicks and scratches from stinging branches, Lisa couldn't find any problems.

When she had finally convinced herself that the mare was unhurt, Lisa breathed a sigh of relief. They had been lucky this time. Then she glanced back the way they had come. The underbrush was trampled flat, showing where they had passed.

"At least you left us a clear trail to follow back," Lisa commented with relief. Even though she knew they couldn't be far from Pine Hollow, Lisa also knew that it was all too easy to get lost in these woods if you didn't know where you were going. Prancer could easily find her own way back, but her instincts would lead her to travel as the crow flies. Anything from perilous rocky areas to impassable thickets to deep sections of Willow Creek might lie between the horse and the stable at this point. There was even a bog somewhere in these woods, Lisa knew. She didn't want to deal with those sorts of barriers if she didn't have to. It would be safer simply to follow the trail they'd made, even if it wasn't the most direct route.

At that moment Lisa felt a heavy drop of rain hit her arm. She glanced up, and another droplet hit her square on the forehead. The rain that had been threatening all day was finally starting.

"Uh-oh," she said.

The drops started coming harder and faster, beating a steady staccato against the piles of dead autumn leaves that coated the ground. But then another noise became audible

—hoofbeats approaching. Seconds later Nero and Dinah emerged from the woods.

Lisa's jaw dropped. She couldn't believe Dinah had followed Prancer. In her place, Lisa herself would have returned to Pine Hollow for help. That was the most sensible course of action, since there was no way Nero would have been able to catch up to the fleet former racehorse. Luckily, since both Lisa and Prancer were unhurt, there was no harm done. Still, Lisa couldn't help being more annoyed with Dinah than ever. Didn't she ever stop to think before she acted?

"Are you okay?" Dinah called when she spotted Lisa.

Lisa nodded. "I think so," she said, trying not to sound as upset as she felt. The wild ride had unnerved her—the last thing she felt like doing right now was chatting with Dinah. "Prancer is, too."

"That's good," Dinah replied, dismounting and glancing at Prancer. "Boy, can she run. I can't believe you stayed on her."

That was all Lisa could take. "Oh, really?" she cried, her voice uncharacteristically loud and shrill. "Well, believe it, okay? I know I haven't been riding as long as you have, but you don't have to act all surprised and make a big deal out of it every time I do something right!"

Dinah looked surprised for a moment, then angry. "Hey, don't yell at me," she said sharply. "I was trying to compliment you. What's your problem?"

"What's *my* problem?" Lisa shrieked in disbelief. Now

that she had started, all her pent-up anger from the past few days came flooding out. She blinked to clear the raindrops from her eyes. The rain was gaining strength and intensity along with her anger. "What's *my* problem? You should ask yourself that same question! All you've done since you got here is insult me and make fun of me in front of my best friends!"

"What?" Dinah exclaimed, her face reddening. She took a step forward, slipping and almost falling on the leaves, which were becoming slick and soggy in the rain. "Don't blame me just because you can't take a joke!"

"Oh yeah?" Lisa yelled back. "Well if you ask me, *you're* the joke. All you can do is make fun of everything and everybody. You don't ever stop joking around long enough to notice when people don't think you're funny. In fact, you don't even have enough sense to go for help when somebody's horse runs away with them."

"Well, I guess I'd better take some lessons from you then, O Great Teacher," Dinah said sarcastically. "After all, you do know everything about everything." Putting her hands on her hips, she glared at Lisa. "The next thing you know, you'll be blaming me for Prancer's running away, too."

Lisa pushed a lock of dripping-wet hair out of her eyes and glared back. At that moment she hated everything about Dinah—her perky attitude, her jokes, her face. She hated the fact that Dinah had known Stevie and Carole longer than she had. She especially hated the fact that Stevie and Carole both liked Dinah so much. She hated that Mrs. Reg had forced her to ride with Dinah today, and she hated the fact that Dinah was standing in front of her right now. She even hated that stupid Paul Revere costume Dinah was wearing, which was now plastered to her, thanks to the rain. Lisa thought Dinah looked more like a soggy red, white, and blue drowning victim than like a Revolutionary War hero.

The costumes, the rain, the runaway horse—everything seemed reduced to little knots of anger and frustration. Nothing was going right, and just then nothing seemed as if it ever would go right.

The two girls faced one another glumly, separated by a few feet of woodland and a giant chasm of feeling.

"If Stevie were here, she'd be laughing," Lisa said. "I mean, you look pretty funny. I bet I do, too."

"More like a city slicker than a cowgirl," Dinah confirmed.

"More like a drowned rat than Paul Revere," Lisa informed her.

"I probably look as if I'd gone by sea instead of the redcoats," Dinah suggested.

"Without a boat," Lisa agreed.

That made Dinah laugh. She had a nice laugh—warm, hearty, inviting. Lisa began to laugh, too. Maybe they did have something in common after all.

"WE PROBABLY SHOULDN'T tell anyone that we didn't even have enough sense to get in out of the rain," Dinah said a few minutes later. It was still raining, but now the two girls and their horses were drying off beneath a deep rock overhang at the edge of the clearing. It was several dozen yards wide and just high enough to allow the horses to stand upright. Most importantly, it was dry.

Lisa wrung out her bandanna and tied it back around her neck. She shivered. "You're right," she agreed. "Although we'll both probably end up with pneumonia as a reminder not to do it again."

Dinah sat down on a rock near the front of the little cave and stared out at the rain, which was pouring down steadily.

"It's too bad it had to rain on the kids' treasure hunt," she commented.

"Not to mention on us," Lisa added.

Dinah laughed. "No kidding."

Lisa smiled. She couldn't believe it. She and Dinah were having a real conversation, just like real friends. Had she misjudged Dinah all along? She was beginning to have the funniest feeling that she might have. She sat down next to the other girl. The rain didn't show any sign of letting up.

"If there's anyone more annoyed than us about this, though, it's got to be Stevie," Dinah continued. "She's probably yelling at the clouds right now for raining on her treasure hunt."

Lisa chuckled at the thought. That sounded just like Stevie. "You do know her pretty well," she told Dinah. She gave her a sidelong glance. "I guess maybe a little better than I was expecting," she added softly.

"What do you mean?" Dinah asked, looking puzzled.

Lisa shrugged. "I don't know, really," she said. "It's just that I'm so used to thinking of Stevie and Carole and me as being each other's best friends that I sort of forgot for a while that we're not each other's *only* friends."

"So when I showed up and you saw how much fun Stevie and I had together—" Dinah began.

"I guess I got a little jealous," Lisa admitted. "I mean, part of what makes my friendship with Stevie so great is that we're so different from one another. But on the other hand, I sometimes feel like she could have more fun with someone more like her—someone like you. I thought she might start to like you better than me. Pretty silly, huh?"

"Not really," Dinah said with a wry smile. "I have to admit I was a little jealous of you, too."

"For being friends with Stevie?" Lisa said, surprised.

Dinah shook her head. "I was expecting that," she said. "Stevie talked about you and Carole the whole time she was visiting me. So I knew about that part. But I also knew that you haven't been riding as long as I have. So when I got here and all anyone could talk about was what a superstar you are, I got a little annoyed."

"I'm not really a superstar, but I guess I can see your point," Lisa said slowly. "I guess I talked about the riding lesson thing a lot when you first arrived."

"It isn't your fault," Dinah said. "You were fine. I can see that now. It's just that even though I love riding, it doesn't come as naturally to me as it does to some people, like you and Stevie and Carole. I don't know if I don't work as hard or if it's just one of those things you're either born with or you're not. But when I got here and kept hearing about what a natural you were, it reminded me of what I'm not. And I took it out on you."

Lisa had to think about that for a minute. She never took her riding ability for granted—she had worked too hard at it. But over the years plenty of other people, from teachers to friends to total strangers, had complimented her on her ability to do almost anything she set her mind to. People kept telling her that she was smarter and more talented than average, but this was the first time she had really stopped to think about what that meant. In this case, it meant that she had unintentionally hurt Dinah's feelings. It wasn't really her fault and it wasn't really Dinah's. It just was.

"Well, I'm just glad we both finally realized what we didn't like," Lisa said at last. "It wasn't each other. It was more like something in ourselves."

Dinah looked thoughtful, then nodded. "You know, I think you really are as smart as Stevie always said you were," she said. And this time Lisa knew the compliment was sincere.

She decided it was time for a change of subject. "So aside from all that, have you had fun in Willow Creek?" she asked.

"Definitely," Dinah said. "Going back to Fenton Hall was a blast, and of course being at Pine Hollow has been even better. I didn't realize how much I missed Max and Mrs. Reg and the horses until I got here. And it's great to finally meet some of the new horses I've heard so much about, like Belle and Starlight." She paused for a second. "And then there's Black Magic, of course."

Lisa grimaced. She had forgotten all about Stevie's little prank. After a short struggle with her conscience, she took a deep breath. "Look, Dinah," she began. "I feel like I'm about to be really disloyal to Stevie, but I think there's something you should know—"

Dinah raised a hand to stop her. "Don't bother," she said.

"I've known for days that there's no such horse at Pine Hollow."

"You have?" Lisa asked, astonished.

"Of course," Dinah said with a grin. She folded her arms across her chest and leaned back. "Stevie should know better than to try to trick me with something so obvious. I suspected something was up from the beginning. Special shoes, my foot!"

"And when did you know for sure?"

"When Phil confirmed my suspicions," Dinah admitted. "That's when I decided to do what I've been doing—stringing Stevie along and driving her crazy by bugging her about Black Magic every chance I get."

Lisa laughed. "You two really are two of a kind," she exclaimed. "That sounds just like something Stevie would do if the tables were turned!" Just then she glanced outside their shelter and noticed that the rain seemed to be tapering off.

Dinah followed her gaze. "Do you think we should try to head back now?" she said. "This may be the best chance we get before it starts to get dark."

"You're right," Lisa said. "Anyway, it looks as though it might actually stop. Should we try to follow the trail?"

Dinah got up and walked across the clearing to where the horses had entered it. "That might be easier said than done," she remarked. "The rain has pretty much washed it away."

"Oh, no!" Lisa said, her heart sinking. She joined Dinah

and gazed into the woods. "I think we might still be able to do it if we go slowly," she said, biting her lip.

"Why bother?" Dinah said. "Let's just let the horses find the way home. That'll be faster."

"Sure it will," Lisa said. "Unless they lead us to the edge of a ravine or straight through a bramble patch or something. We know the trail is pretty clear. I think we should stick to it."

Dinah shook her head. "You were moving too fast to notice, but I can tell you, the trail was hard to follow in spots even before it rained. Prancer didn't stop to mark the way, and she crossed all kinds of clearings. It could take us hours to search out the right way."

Lisa shrugged. "All right, you win," she said. "Let's let Nero lead." As she followed Dinah back to the overhang to fetch the horses, Lisa couldn't help smiling. An hour ago she would have been outraged to have lost an argument with Dinah. But now she didn't mind at all.

Dinah was obviously thinking the same thing. "See? That didn't hurt, did it?" she teased, giving Lisa a sidelong glance.

Lisa smiled as she tightened Prancer's girth. "Not a bit," she said.

As soon as Nero realized what was being asked of him, he set off confidently along a narrow trail just to the east of the one Prancer had made during her wild run. The girls settled back and rode in companionable silence for a while, letting Nero lead the way.

Something was still bothering Lisa, though. Even though

Carole had thought Lisa's suspicions of Dinah and Phil were caused by Lisa's dislike of Dinah, Lisa knew that wasn't the whole story. She really had caught the pair acting suspiciously a couple of times, and she wanted to know why. What had they really been up to?

The last thing Lisa wanted to do was make Dinah mad again. She would have to be tactful. "So, Dinah," she began casually as they rode side by side across a grassy clearing. "I'm glad you found out about Black Magic, but I'm a little surprised at Phil. After all, he is Stevie's boyfriend—I wonder why he decided to give away her secret?"

Dinah blushed and glanced at Lisa. "Well, I guess it wouldn't hurt to tell you. . . ."

As Lisa and Dinah rode across the field behind Pine Hollow a few minutes later, they saw Max waving to them.

"I was about to send out a search party," he said when they reached the stable yard. "Everyone else came back when it started to rain." He cast a glance over the girls' hair and costumes, which were still soaked. "I guess you two didn't quite make it."

"Not quite," Lisa said ruefully, dismounting. "Who won the treasure hunt?"

"I don't know. But I think Stevie is about to make the grand announcement inside," Max replied. He reached for Prancer's and Nero's reins. "I'll take the horses in while you go get yourselves cleaned up."

"Thanks, Max," Lisa and Dinah said in one voice. They

went inside and found the kids gathered in the locker area. Stevie and Phil were at the front of the room near the costume box sifting through a pile of slightly soggy treasure.

"Oh, there you two are!" Carole exclaimed as soon as she saw Lisa and Dinah enter. "We were getting worried. Phil said you were having some trouble with Prancer on the trail."

"That's an understatement," Lisa said. "But don't worry. Everything turned out fine." She glanced at Dinah and smiled. Dinah smiled back.

Carole noticed the exchange, and her eyes widened. But she decided not to say anything. She was sure Lisa would tell her the whole story later. Right now it was time to listen to Stevie's big announcement.

"I've added up the booty that each team brought back," Stevie said, raising her hands for quiet. "And we have a winner. The winning team in the Great Pine Hollow Treasure Hunt is—the Ghouls!"

Phil, Joe, and the other team members cheered loudly.

"Come on up and get your prize, Ghouls," Stevie called. "First pick of costumes!"

Within minutes the three kids were wearing their costumes. One little girl was a ballerina, another was a ghost, and Joe, of course, was a pirate.

Then Stevie called up the rest of the groups one by one to choose. Before long, a vampire, a doctor, a mummy, three witches, a space alien, and two very short Marines were added to the crowd.

112

Carole, Lisa, and Dinah joined Stevie as she peered into the now almost empty box. "I don't think Joe had to worry about getting a pirate costume," Stevie commented. "There must still be enough for at least half a dozen pirates in here, thanks to my brothers' originality."

Dinah looked into the box and saw that it still contained several other items, too—including a cowboy hat. She looked at Lisa with a grin.

"Are you thinking what I'm thinking?" Lisa asked.

"I am if you're thinking we could salvage these wet costumes we have on," Dinah replied.

The others watched as Lisa and Dinah dug out new costumes for themselves. Soon they wore new and improved cowgirl and Paul Revere costumes.

Joe spotted them and came running over. "Hey!" he cried, brandishing his cardboard sword. "Where have you been?"

"Oh, just out and about," Dinah said. "But we got back just in time to see you win. Your pirate costume looks great."

"Thanks." Joe looked at Lisa solemnly. "I'm sorry I scared your horse before."

"Apology accepted," Lisa said with a smile. "Don't worry, Dinah came and rescued us."

When Joe ran off to rejoin his friends, Carole leaned closer to Lisa. "You and Dinah must have had a very interesting ride," she commented quietly.

Lisa nodded. She glanced around and saw that Stevie was

busy talking to Phil and Dinah. "As a matter of fact, I have something to tell you about that. . . ."

"So, Stevie," Dinah was saying at that same moment. "Do you think Max will bring Black Magic back here before I leave tomorrow? I really do want to see her before I go."

"I'm sure he will," Stevie said.

"Good," Dinah said. "Maybe we should come back first thing in the morning. My plane leaves pretty early, you know."

Before Stevie could respond, Mrs. Reg stuck her head in. "Everybody back outside," she called. "The rain has stopped; it's a beautiful, warm evening; and best of all, it's time to eat!"

The kids, younger and older, let out a cheer. The day had been fun and full of activity, and now everyone was hungry. They hurried outside to find Max and Red working the grill. Several large plastic tablecloths served as picnic blankets on the wet ground nearby, and sodas were chilling in a cooler under a tree.

"Mmm, there's nothing like a grilled burger when you're really hungry," Stevie declared a few minutes later as she joined her friends on a blanket near the outdoor ring. Draping her Betsy Ross flag over the fence, she picked up her hamburger with both hands. She took a big bite and chewed happily. The burger was hot and juicy and cooked medium-rare, just the way she liked it.

"That's for sure," Phil said. He tipped his soda can to his mouth, draining the last few drops. Then he wiped his mouth and stood up. "Boy, am I thirsty. I'm going to get another. Want to come, Stevie?"

Stevie blushed and stood up. She was sure Phil was just trying to come up with an excuse to get her to take a walk with him. They had been so busy all day that they hadn't had much time alone. Deciding her appetite could wait a few more minutes, she set down her burger and stood up.

"This has been a really fun day," Phil commented as the pair strolled slowly among blankets full of happy kids toward the cooler. "I think these kids will remember it for a long time."

"I hope so," Stevie said. "I hope they can come back again sometime, too."

"That would be great," Phil said. "I'm going to tell Mr. Baker about this; maybe Cross County could sponsor something like this, too." That was the name of Phil's Pony Club. Mr. Baker was his riding instructor.

Stevie smiled. It was wonderful having a boyfriend as nice, smart, and fun as Phil. And it was even more wonderful to know that he cared about the same kinds of things that she did—things like making sure these kids had fun today and wanting to help them in any other way he could.

Lisa, Carole, and Dinah were still eating when Stevie and Phil returned. The three of them were sitting in a row at the edge of the blanket, watching and laughing as one of the Marines tried to get the vampire and two of the witches to line up and salute. He wasn't having much luck.

Stevie sat down behind Carole and grabbed her plate.

The walk with Phil had been nice, but she had to admit she was glad to return to her meal. Phil sat down beside her and picked up his own hamburger. He took a bite.

"That hits the spot," he commented through a mouthful of food.

Stevie nodded and eagerly bit into her own bun. But a second later she wrinkled her nose, then quickly grabbed a napkin and spat out what she had just bitten. "Oh, yuck!" she cried as soon as she could speak.

Carole, Lisa, and Dinah turned around. "What is it, Stevie?" Lisa asked, looking concerned.

Stevie waved her hand at her plate with a look of disgust. "My hamburger!" she exclaimed.

"Did a bug get in it?" Carole asked sympathetically. "I hate when that happens. It's the only bad thing about picnics."

"No, a bug did not get in it," Stevie replied, peeling back the bun.

Dinah peered at the burger. "It looks a little funny," she commented.

"Well, it tastes even funnier," Stevie said. "Although Belle might disagree. It tastes just like what she usually has for dinner. Somebody replaced my delicious hamburger with a bunful of grain!"

Carole gasped. "What?" she exclaimed. "But you were only gone for a minute! And the three of us were here the whole time!"

"Well, we were here, but we weren't really watching

Stevie's plate," Lisa reminded her. "Our backs were to it. Anyone or anything could have switched the burger without our noticing."

"Almost anyone," Stevie muttered. This proved it beyond a shadow of doubt: This time it couldn't possibly have been Phil, no matter what. But if not Phil, who? It was all completely mystifying—unless, of course, the stable really had a poltergeist. . . .

As THE SKY grew darker and stars appeared between the patches of cloud that still hung in the sky, the group moved indoors once again. It was time for Phil's magic show.

"Come one, come all!" Dinah called out as the kids filed into the indoor ring. It had been magically transformed into a magician's theater. Phil and Dinah had cut silvery moons, stars, and other shapes out of aluminum foil and hung them on the walls. Flickering candles in glass jars cast mysterious shadows everywhere. The edges of the makeshift stage were marked by two tall stacks of hay bales covered with black fabric, and in the center of the stage area was a table covered with a shiny blue cloth and containing a variety of objects, including a tall, black top hat. "Come and be amazed, come and be confounded, by the one and only, magical, mystical, Magnificent Marsteno!"

Phil stepped forward with a flourish and gave a low bow. His long red-lined black cape billowed behind him as he strode toward the table to begin his first trick—pulling a bridle out of his hat.

When he finished that, Dinah stepped forward to take the bridle from him while the kids cheered loudly. Dinah stepped back to the edge of the stage.

"Pretty cool trick, huh?" Dinah said to Carole, Stevie, and Lisa, who were watching from behind the hay bales.

"I'll say," Carole agreed. "There's no way that bridle could have fit inside that hat even if he hadn't shown us it was empty. How did he do it?"

Dinah grinned. "Are you kidding? That's his best trick. He'd kill me if I told you," she said. "Besides, it's kind of complicated. But watch this—there's an easier one coming up. After it's done I'll tell you how he did it."

The others watched as Phil picked up a banana from the table.

"Boy, that first trick sure made me hungry!" he announced to his audience. "I think I'll have a banana. But I like my banana sliced into bite-size pieces."

He reached down to the table and pretended to pick something up.

"What are you doing?" called out Joe, who was sitting in the front row watching Phil's every move carefully. "There's nothing there!"

"Ah, but there is," Phil said, holding up his hand. "This is my invisible knife."

"There's no such thing!" yelled a girl near the back of the group.

"Yes, there certainly is," Phil said. "And the most important thing to know about an invisible knife is that it can cut through this banana *without* cutting through the skin." He gestured to Joe. "Why don't you come up here and help me?"

Joe jumped to his feet and hurried forward. "I still don't see any knife," he said, staring at Phil's empty hand.

Phil held up the banana. "Now watch carefully," he instructed Joe. "I'm going to cut it in four pieces. That's how I like to eat it."

With Joe watching his every move, Phil slowly pretended to slice the banana into four equal sections with his invisible knife.

"Okay, it's ready now," he said. "I've cut it up inside the skin." He handed the banana to Joe. "Why don't you peel it for me?"

Joe took the banana. After carefully examining the skin to make sure it was still intact, he peeled the banana. He gasped. "Hey! It *is* cut up already!" he exclaimed, holding it up to show the other kids. Then he turned back to Phil. "How did you do that?"

Phil shrugged and reached for one of the banana sections. "I told you," he said popping it into his mouth. "Invisible knife."

While the kids applauded, Stevie turned to Dinah. "Okay, let's hear it," she said. "How did he do that?"

"Like I said, that's actually a pretty easy one," Dinah said with a grin. "All we had to do was prepare the banana beforehand by sticking a needle through the skin in three different spots and wiggling it back and forth so that it sliced through the banana. There's no way the audience would notice the tiny needle holes in the skin. So when the banana is peeled it seems like magic."

The others laughed. "What a great trick!" Stevie exclaimed. "I think I'll try it at school on Monday. Now, I'll just have to figure out where to hide the needle. . . ."

Dinah grinned. "I'm sorry I'll miss it." She glanced back at the stage, where Phil was in the midst of a trick using a handkerchief and a coin. "In a minute I get to do my first solo trick," she said.

"What is it?" Lisa asked.

"I'm going to make a riding crop seem to stick to my hand," Dinah replied. She held up her left hand with her fingers spread and the palm facing away from the other girls. Then she wrapped her right hand around her left wrist so that the fingers and thumb met over the back of her left hand. "See, I only let the audience see the back of my left hand," she explained. "Meanwhile, they'll think my right hand is just holding my wrist, but really my index finger will be stretched out to my palm, holding the crop against it. But the audience won't see that finger because it's behind my wrist. And if I play it right they'll never notice that only three of the fingers and the thumb on my right hand are showing." She pulled a riding crop out of her pocket and demonstrated. It did look just as though the crop were attached to her hand with nothing holding it there. "I'll shake my hand as if I'm trying to get rid of the crop—but of course I'll be holding on to it with my right-hand index finger the whole time. See, the hardest part of each trick is the acting. You have to make the audience believe that the impossible things they're seeing are really happening."

"Well, Phil is awfully good at that part, that's for sure," Carole said admiringly. "He almost had me convinced with that invisible knife business."

Just then Phil finished another trick. After the applause died down, he clapped his hands. "And now, my talented assistant, Dinah the Dynamic, will bring me a riding crop for my next trick."

Dinah winked at her friends and hurried out, holding the crop. The kids shrieked with laughter as she pretended the crop was stuck to her hand. Phil did a very convincing job of pretending to yank on it with all his might, while Dinah herself frantically tried to shake it loose.

Suddenly Stevie remembered something. She had hung her Betsy Ross flag on the fence of the outdoor ring during dinner and never picked it up afterward. Stevie had solemnly sworn to her mother that she would take good care of it. If it rained again and the flag got soaked, Mrs. Lake might never forgive her. Stevie sighed. She hated to miss even a few minutes of the magic show, but she knew she would hate being grounded for life much more. "I'll be right back," she whispered to Carole.

Carole just nodded, her eyes glued to Phil, who was now pretending to put a spell on the riding crop so that it would let go of Dinah.

Stevie crept out of the indoor ring quietly, not wanting to

distract the kids from Phil's act. She needn't have worried, though—Phil's audience was completely engrossed. Stevie was glad to see that the kids were having fun. All kids deserved to have fun, no matter how poor they were or where they lived. And to have fun with horses around— that was even better, in Stevie's opinion.

Outside, Stevie quickly spotted her flag still hanging on the fence where she'd left it. She grabbed it and hurried back inside, shivering a little. The sun had gone down and the air was damp and chilly.

As she was heading back toward the indoor ring, Stevie heard a familiar whinny. She turned down the aisle and went to Belle's stall. The mare was looking out over the half door.

"Hi, girl," Stevie whispered, giving her a pat. Then she gasped. Someone had braided the horse's mane! The neat rows of dark hair were plaited with black and orange ribbons. The ends fluttered gaily in the air.

Stevie fingered the tight braids. Then she slipped inside the stall to get a look at the mare's tail. Sure enough, it was also braided with black and orange ribbons, looking neat and trim enough to step out in a show—a Halloween show.

"But who?" Stevie muttered. Who could have done this? She was already convinced that Phil wasn't the poltergeist, and this proved it once again. He and Dinah had been busy setting up in the indoor ring the last time Stevie had seen Belle. And although for one crazy moment Stevie suspected Carole simply because the braider had done such a professional job, she knew that Carole couldn't have done it either. For one thing, Carole hadn't been out of Stevie's sight for more than five minutes at a time for the last couple of hours, and this braiding job had certainly taken a lot more than five minutes. For another thing, Stevie was sure that Carole wasn't the poltergeist. It wasn't like her. And besides, she hadn't even been around when some of the pranks had happened—the first appearance of the poltergeist book, for instance.

Stevie sighed and gave Belle a farewell pat. "Well, if a poltergeist did this, he sure knows what he's doing," she told the horse. "He could get a job with any stable in the country."

She turned and walked back to the indoor ring, arriving just in time for Phil's grand finale. She watched as he made a series of objects disappear inside a big red horse blanket, then made them reappear again throughout the audience. It was an impressive trick, but Stevie wasn't really concentrating on it. She was too busy thinking about an even more mysterious trick—Belle's braided mane and tail. She knew it had taken more than sleight of hand to do that. It had taken know-how and, more importantly, time.

"Okay, everyone," Max said, stepping forward after Phil had finished. "Let's have a big hand for the Magnificent Marsteno and his talented assistant, Dinah the Dynamic."

The kids cheered loud and long. Stevie could tell they had all loved the show, and she felt proud of Phil.

"And now," Max continued, "it's time for something special. Who wants to go trick-or-treating?"

Every hand in the place went up, including Stevie's, Carole's, Lisa's, Dinah's, and Phil's.

"Come on," Carole said to her friends. "Let's go get saddled up." Since Mr. Toll's hay wagon wasn't large enough for everyone, most of the Pine Hollow students were going to ride alongside it on their horses. They hurried away to get ready.

A few minutes later, everyone gathered outside the stable entrance. Carole glanced at Belle's mane and tail, which were still braided with the bright Halloween ribbons.

"Nice look for Belle, Stevie," she commented. "When did you do it?"

Stevie bit her lip. "Oh, yeah—um—thanks," she said, avoiding the question. She didn't want to go into details about the poltergeist's latest trick right now—not until she'd figured out who had done it.

"Is Mr. Toll here yet?" Lisa asked Max.

"He should be arriving any minute," Max replied, glancing at his watch.

As if on cue, a jingling sound came from the road. A moment later the wagon rolled into sight. Mr. Toll was sitting in front, holding the long reins with which he drove his team—a perfectly matched pair of sturdy black workhorses. The horses trotted up the drive and stopped in front of the waiting crowd. Mr. Toll climbed down from his perch and went to greet Max.

Meanwhile, Stevie grabbed Dinah by the arm and pulled her forward. "What a lucky break!" she exclaimed.

"What?" Dinah asked, looking confused.

Carole and Lisa were confused, too. They exchanged a glance and followed Stevie and Dinah toward the wagon. Phil was right behind them.

"This is her!" Stevie walked up to one of the black work-horses and laid a hand on its huge neck. "It's Black Magic! Isn't she wonderful?"

Carole and Lisa gasped. So this was what Stevie had planned to humiliate Dinah!

But Dinah didn't miss a beat. She rushed forward. "Oh, yes!" she squealed, reaching up to pat the gigantic mare on her nose. "She's everything you said she was, Stevie! No, she's even more wonderful than you said she was. Why, I think she's the most beautiful horse I've ever seen in my life!"

Stevie looked confused for a second, then started to look annoyed. She was beginning to have the funniest feeling that *she* was the one who had been had, not Dinah—especially since the rest of her friends were giggling wildly. "But —but—" she sputtered. "You mean you *knew?*"

"I don't know what you're talking about, Stevie," Dinah said innocently, flinging an arm around Black Magic's neck. The horse was so big that she had to stand on tiptoes to do it. "You've been telling me all week long about this incredible horse, and now here she is."

125

Carole grinned. "She's got you there, Stevie," she said. "You can't tell me that this big girl isn't pretty incredible."

Stevie pouted for a second, then smiled. "I guess you're right," she admitted, giving Black Magic another pat. Then she joined in the laughter. Even though the joke had been on her, it had been pretty funny, and Stevie could certainly appreciate that.

"Come on, everyone," Max called to them. "It's time to go."

The Saddle Club and their friends hurried to mount their horses, which were waiting patiently near the ring, while the visiting kids clambered into the soft, scratchy piles of hay in the back of Mr. Toll's wagon.

"Ready when you are, Mr. Toll," Max called.

The old farmer nodded and took his position in the driver's seat. "We're off, then," he said gruffly. With a flick of the reins, he clucked to his team, and the two big horses stepped off into the cool evening.

"Look at the mist," Lisa commented to Carole as they rode after the wagon at a walk.

Carole looked around at the wispy gray mist that floated just above the ground all around them, a reminder of the damp, rainy weather they'd been having. "It's pretty spooky-looking, isn't it?" she commented.

Stevie overheard. "Perfect trick-or-treating weather!" she declared happily.

THE FOLLOWING DAY passed quickly. First Dinah left for the airport, after promising Stevie, Carole, and Lisa that she would return soon for another visit. She also invited all of them to visit her in Vermont anytime.

Then it was time to return to Pine Hollow. After the trick-or-treating hayride the evening before, the exhausted but happy city kids had climbed back onto their bus, clutching bags of candy and other goodies and mumbling sleepy good-byes to their hosts. Max had sent the older kids home soon afterward, after extracting promises from them all that they would return the next day to help clean up.

He had meant it, too. As soon as The Saddle Club arrived, he put them to work. The three girls barely had a chance to exchange a word for the next several hours, let alone discuss the events of the day before.

So when the work was finally finished and Stevie announced, "Saddle Club meeting—TD's," her friends eagerly agreed. Fifteen minutes later the girls were seated in their favorite booth at Tastee Delight, the local ice cream parlor.

While they waited for the waitress to come and take their order, Stevie pulled the poltergeist book out of her pocket and began to flip through it idly. "You know, I still can't figure out this whole poltergeist thing," she admitted. "I was so sure it was Phil at first. He could have done some of the tricks, like the cats in the tack room and the currycombs in my locker. But then I realized that there were lots of others he couldn't possibly have done. He wasn't around when the saddle soap disappeared, or when this poltergeist book first turned up on the chair. And then there was the falling hard hats—he wasn't there that day, either. And, of course, that disgusting grain burger."

Stevie paused when she saw the waitress approaching.

"What will you have, girls?" the waitress asked, pulling out her pad and giving Stevie a resigned look. Stevie was famous for the strange and often disgusting combinations of ice cream she ordered.

Stevie didn't disappoint the waitress this time. "I'll have a Stevie Lake Halloween special," she announced.

The waitress just raised an eyebrow and waited.

"That's orange sherbet and black licorice ice cream,"

128

Stevie continued. "With some ghostly white marshmallow topping. And, of course, a cherry on top."

The waitress wrote it all down, trying not to grimace. Then she quickly took Carole's and Lisa's orders and hurried away without another word.

Stevie immediately returned to her previous topic. "So if it wasn't Phil, who was it?" she said. "I couldn't figure it out. For a while I thought it might have been Dinah—after all, she had the motive, and she could have done some of the pranks. She could have planted the book and the chair when she said she was going to the bathroom. And she could have done the currycomb thing just as easily as Phil." Stevie shrugged. "But then I remembered that she hadn't even arrived yet when the saddle soap disappeared. And she couldn't have rounded up all those cats—she wasn't out of my sight at all before that happened. Besides, she and Phil were both busy with the magic show during the last couple of pranks."

"So who do you think it was?" Carole asked.

"Yeah, who?" Lisa added.

Stevie was gazing into space thoughtfully, so she didn't notice the unusually mischievous twinkle in her friends' eyes. "I just don't know," she muttered. "It really bugs me. I can't think of one person who could have pulled off all those crazy pranks."

"Maybe it wasn't one person," Lisa suggested meaningfully.

Stevie sighed. "Don't start with that poltergeist stuff,"

she said. "Even if I can't figure out who did it, I still am not going to believe it was some troublemaking ghost."

"I don't think that's what Lisa meant, Stevie," Carole said with a giggle. "She didn't mean it wasn't one *person*. She meant it wasn't one person."

By this time Lisa was giggling too. Stevie stared blankly from one to the other of her friends for a moment. Then a look of realization dawned on her face. "You mean, you two were in on it together?" she exclaimed.

"Not just us," Lisa said. "Us—*and* Phil and Dinah."

Stevie smacked herself on the forehead. "I can't believe it!" she exclaimed. "You all ganged up on me?"

"Well, not at first," Carole said. "At first it was just Phil. But when he realized you were on to him, he enlisted Dinah's help. He figured you would never suspect that the two of them were working together since they'd just met."

"He was right," Stevie admitted. "I never would have thought they were working on anything together except the magic show."

"Of course not," Carole said, giving Lisa a meaningful glance. "Nobody would."

Lisa blushed. She knew Carole was thinking of Lisa's suspicions about Phil and Dinah.

Luckily Stevie didn't notice a thing. She was busy thinking back over all the pranks that had occurred during the past week and figuring out who had been responsible for each one.

"So I guess Phil must have been behind the black cat trick," she said.

Carole nodded. "He got to Pine Hollow earlier than you thought he did and rounded up all the cats. Then he came into the locker room, pretending he had just arrived, and came up with an excuse to send you to the tack room."

"That rat!" Stevie exclaimed. "What about the book? I suppose that had to have been Dinah. She must have bought it at the mall when I was waiting in line at the pizza place. Then she planted it while I thought she was in the bathroom."

"Lucky for her the mall was so crowded," Lisa commented. "Otherwise she might have had more trouble with that one."

"Then I guess they just took turns stealing the book back and then leaving it in strange places, like Belle's stall," Stevie said, thinking back. "And Dinah must have knocked down those hats. And either she or Phil must have stuffed my locker with those currycombs."

"Phil," Carole confirmed, "with Dinah standing guard at the door to distract anyone who happened by. Phil was also the one who hung the bridles upside down, by the way." She grinned. "See, the hardest part of each trick is the acting. You have to make your audience believe the impossible things they're seeing are really happening."

"Very funny," Stevie said dryly, remembering that Dinah had said the same thing during Phil's magic act. It was true, though. Her friends had done such a good acting job that

131

Stevie hadn't suspected a thing. "What about the rest of the pranks?"

"Well, Phil left Mrs. Reg's phone in Belle's feed box," Lisa said. "I kind of ruined that one. I wasn't in on the joke yet, so when I found the phone I just returned it and forgot to even mention it to you."

"And the grain burger?" Stevie asked, making a face as she remembered the taste.

Lisa giggled. "That's where Carole and I came in," she said. "When Dinah and I were riding back to Pine Hollow after the treasure hunt, she told me she and Phil had been behind all the pranks. So I told Carole, we made up a fake burger while Phil kept you out of the way for a few minutes, and the rest is history."

"Well, almost," Stevie said, giving Lisa a sidelong glance. "I'm still waiting to hear what happened out there during that rainstorm. All I know is that you and Dinah were practically at each other's throats all week, and then presto —you're best friends."

"Well, it wasn't quite that simple," Lisa said. Taking a deep breath, she told Stevie and Carole the whole story. "So once Dinah and I started over, we got along fine," she finished.

"It's almost like Prancer ran away on purpose," Carole said. "You know, to get you two to be friends."

Stevie rolled her eyes. "Come on, Carole."

"Well, okay, maybe not," Carole admitted. "But you have to admit, horses did bring Lisa and Dinah together. I always suspected that horses could solve almost any problem, and in this case it was true. And never mind about poltergeists and all that other mysterious stuff. What I'm talking about is horse magic. That's the best kind of magic there is."

Lisa couldn't help agreeing with that. "Although I think 'horse magic' is just another name for 'friendship,'" she pointed out. "Or should that be the other way around?"

"Well, whatever it is, I'm glad we've got it," Stevie said. "After all, it was horse magic that brought The Saddle Club together."

"True," Lisa said. "And that's another thing I wanted to tell you guys. After making up with Dinah and hearing her point of view about things, I realized more than ever how great The Saddle Club really is." She paused and smiled at Stevie. "Although I have to admit that I'm glad there's only one major practical joker in the group!"

Stevie grinned back. "Well, I don't know about that," she said. "You guys seem to be catching up." She paused and glanced down at the poltergeist book. "There's still a couple of tricks I can't figure out," she admitted.

"Which ones?" asked Carole.

"The disappearing soap, and the braided mane and tail," Stevie said. "*Especially* the braided mane and tail. When I stopped by Belle's stall during the magic show, someone had braided her mane and tail with those ribbons you saw. But all four of you guys were present and accounted for during the time it had to have been done. So who did it?"

Lisa grinned. "Hmmm . . . must have been that darn poltergeist," she said, shaking her head. "Pesky thing."

Carole nodded. "You know how they are," she added.

"Very funny," Stevie said, crossing her arms.

"Okay, okay," Carole said. "We confess. It wasn't the poltergeist. It was Mrs. Reg."

Stevie gasped. "Mrs. Reg? She was in on this, too?"

"And Max," Lisa confirmed with a nod. "Phil checked with them before he started the whole thing—that's what he was doing when he pretended he'd lost his watch. He knew he'd never get away with it otherwise."

"Those—those sneaky rats," Stevie exclaimed. "So that's why Mrs. Reg told that ridiculous poltergeist story."

"It was also why my dad rented us that movie," Carole said. "He knew about the whole thing even before Lisa and I did, from Max. They figured that if we watched that, we'd get even more crazy ideas about poltergeists."

"I guess we ruined that part of the plan," Lisa said. "We barely made it through the first half hour."

"I can't believe it," Stevie declared.

"What?" asked Lisa. "That we fell asleep?"

"No! That I didn't figure this all out myself," Stevie said, shaking her head.

Carole shrugged. "I guess this means Phil is King of Pranks now, hmm?"

"No way!" Stevie said quickly. "If I hadn't been distracted by that whole Black Magic mess—I suppose I have

Phil to thank for ruining that one, too—I'm sure I would have guessed the truth right away."

"Uh-huh," said Lisa skeptically just as their ice cream arrived. She thanked the waitress, then picked up her spoon and took a bite of her hot fudge sundae.

"No, really," Stevie said. "Anyway, Phil may think he's won now—but not for long."

Carole and Lisa exchanged slightly nervous glances. They recognized that gleam in Stevie's eyes—she was out for revenge. But would she concentrate on Phil or include all of them in her scheme?

"Uh, Stevie," Carole said. "Now that Halloween's over, that means no more pranks until next year, right?"

Stevie didn't answer for a moment. She just smiled, picked up her spoon, and dug into her black-and-orange ice cream concoction. After taking a bite, she finally replied, "Live in fear!"

## ABOUT THE AUTHOR

Bonnie Bryant is the author of nearly a hundred books about horses, including The Saddle Club series, Saddle Club Super Editions, and the Pony Tails series. She has also written novels and movie novelizations under her married name, B. B. Hiller.

Ms. Bryant began writing The Saddle Club in 1986. Although she had done some riding before that, she intensified her studies then and found herself learning right along with her characters Stevie, Carole, and Lisa. She claims that they are all much better riders than she is.

Ms. Bryant was born and raised in New York City. She still lives there, in Greenwich Village, with her two sons.